STRANGLED SKEIN

STITCHES IN CRIME
BOOK 9

ACF BOOKENS

1

———

A friend of mine lives in Austin, and he swears that the summer there is hotter than it is in Virginia. I disagree. While his shoes might melt to the pavement, I sweat through my clothes when I go to take out the trash. Now, I don't want to have to buy new shoes all the time of course, but I would like to not feel like I have to stand in front of the freezer after a simple chore.

It's probably enough to say that my body was not built for Virginia summers. And yet, I love it here, and I love the garden in the summer when everything is beginning to fruit and Sawyer and I can go out and harvest beans and tomatoes before the sun is too far into the sky.

That boy is a gardening machine these days. He grabs my market basket as soon as he has shoes on his feet and heads out, sometimes with me, sometimes with Beauregard, our Maine coon cat. He gathers all the tomatoes, choosing only the reddest ones and not culling our produce by picking everything with fruit like he did last year.

After harvest, we take some for ourselves, some for his grandparents, and some for our friends, and then anything left over – most days we have something left over – we carry our goods up to the small roadside stand we'd set up for our neighbors to display everything for people passing by. I'd left a small jar there that said, "Sawyer's College Fund," and sometimes someone would slip a little cash in there for him. He loved that, but he also loved checking at the end of the day to see what we had "sold." It was a beautiful routine.

On this particular July morning, the tomatoes were thriving, and Sawyer picked a dozen huge beefsteaks and three or four pints of cherries, too. The fruit loved this heat, which made me able to tolerate it, at least until 10 a.m.

Our harvest sorted, he and I walked up to the roadside stand and set out our offerings. Right now besides tomatoes, we mostly had onions and beans, and I was glad to see everything from the day before had been picked up. Plus, Sawyer had $5 in his tip jar. He had been wonderful about keeping that money in his piggy bank and then letting me deposit it every month. And in exchange for his help with the garden, he got a weekly allowance that he got to spend on Matchbox cars and various forms of boomerangs.

As we set out our tomatoes, a pickup truck slowed to a stop in our driveway, and an older man stepped out. "Uncle Saul!" Sawyer shouted as he saw one of my favorite people, my best friend Mika's uncle. "You want some tomatoes?"

"How did you know?" Saul said as he grabbed Sawyer by the arms and swung him around, then set him down in front of the stand. "That's exactly why I stopped."

I had offered Saul free produce over and over again, but true to his nature, he had refused and came regularly to "buy" his own vegetables. I found this endearing for a number of reasons, not the least of which was the fact that he had a thriving garden at his house. Mika said he took the things he bought from us and his own surplus and donated it to the local food pantry.

Today, he picked up two huge tomatoes and deposited a $20 bill in Sawyer's cup. I rolled my eyes at his over-generosity, but I didn't say anything. It would do no good. This was just who Saul was.

"Thanks for these, Saw," he said. "But I'm glad I caught you up here. Saves me from having to use that blasted phone." Saul hated the phone with a surprising vehemence. To me he said, "I have a job for you."

"A salvage job?" I asked. The summer had been kind of quiet on the work front because of the heat and family vacations, and while business at my online and brick-and-mortar stores had been booming, I was feeling anxious about having enough inventory. "What is it?"

He smiled. "You know that old house up north of town, the one covered in ivy?"

"The Sumner Place? They're tearing that down?" The house was in bad shape, but I had always hoped that someone would refurbish it. It was beautiful and old, built around 1790. "That's a shame."

"Oh no, Paisley girl," Saul said. "The new owners are fixing it up. Some folks from DC who want to have a second home down here. They're going all out. Fixing up the outbuildings, too, even plan to redo the slave cabin out back."

"There's a slave quarter still standing?" I felt my heart pick up. "Wow. That's amazing. But what do they need me for if they're going to restore the property?"

His grin grew even wider. "That's the best part. They want you to go through the attic and closets and take anything valuable. Then they'll hire a crew to recycle and trash the rest."

"Whoa, that's amazing. Did you guys talk numbers?" I'd finally learned that I needed to be money conscious, not just opportunity aware, if I wanted my business to thrive.

He nodded and winked. "They are eager to preserve as much of the history as they can, but they also need the house to work for them. So they'd consider it a favor to have you come in and take what you want at no charge."

I stared at him for a minute. "They're going to let me salvage, take anything I want, and not charge me a cent." I shook my head. This had to be too good to be true.

"That's right. There's only one catch."

I sighed, but then I grinned. "They want it done ASAP."

"You got it, girl," Saul said. "Any chance you're available today?"

I looked down at my four-year-old. "What do you think, Saw? You up for some dirty work?"

"Yeah!" he said as he pumped his fist in the air.

"We're in," I said. "Let me just get this guy back to his lair." I scooped up Beau and began to walk down the driveway.

The next two minutes were quite loud in our rural neighborhood as Saw proceeded to honk Saul's horn *all* the way down the driveway back toward the house. I said a silent apology to neighbors near and far and grabbed my keys and wallet after depositing my grouchy cat onto his velour blanket on the sofa. He basically rolled his eyes at me as he forced himself to lay down in utter luxury. Poor guy.

Then, with Saw buckled into his seat in my car and safely away from the truck horn, I followed Saul up north of town to the old house that had been the focus of so many stories through my years growing up here in Octonia. Little kids told stories about a creepy old lady who lived inside and never came out, and when we got to high school, those stories became about ghosts and murders within the walls.

When I'd gotten interested in history in college, I'd done a little research on the house and found that it had been unoccupied since the 1960s, had never been the site of a ghost hunting expedition, and was not the place of record for any murder. That said, it still fascinated me to this day.

The plantation had originally been owned by the Sumner

family, one of the first settlers in Octonia. They'd come up, as had many rich Virginians, from the Tidewater when the king began gifting land to people who would claim it for "king and country." I've always wondered what the Monacan Indians who were the first human occupants of this land had thought of this selling of property they had always lived on but never claimed to own. Surely, the audacity of these White people must have shocked them, to say the least.

Within a few years of getting their land grant, the people the Sumners enslaved had built a small wooden house on the property and cleared much of the land of trees. Then, they had gone to work building the big brick house that was what most of us called the Sumner Place now.

The structure was like so many in Virginia – brick, symmetrical, and columned. I was eager to see the inside, although I imagined it was a traditional two over two (two rooms above and two below) with maybe a central hallway if the Sumners were a little wealthier than most.

As we drove up the lane, I narrated what I could see for Saw, pretending as if he cared. I told him how the layout of the big cedars on either side of the driveway showed that this was the original entrance road and that the horsehead on the pole near the circular driveway meant it was a hitching post for horses. I pointed out the size of the boxwoods out front and said they had probably been put in when the house had been built.

To his credit, my four-year-old proved he'd listened by asking "Can I play in the bot woods?"

I laughed. His pronunciations always made me smile. "I expect so, Saw, but let's meet the people who own the house and ask first, okay?"

My kid, like his mother, loved the smell of boxwoods. My dad Lee thought the shrubs smelled gross, but for me, they smelled like story and home. So as we walked through them with Saul to the front door, I took a deep, deep breath of the scent washing over me.

Before we could even knock on the massive double door at the front of the house, a thin blond woman in a white pantsuit opened the door and said, "Hello! I'm so glad you could come. You must be Paisley." She stepped forward and extended her hand.

"Yes, ma'am. It's nice to meet you. Thank you for this generous offer." I reached back with my free hand to pat my son's back as he hid behind me. "This is Sawyer, my son. He's my apprentice."

"Ooh, learning early, Sawyer. That's wonderful. When you're ready, my nephew Wyatt is here. He's four, and I bet you guys could play together if you'd like."

Saw's wide brown eyes peeked up at me with a question.

"When you're ready, that's just fine with me," I said. Then I turned to the woman, "If you don't mind watching him."

"Don't mind at all. Our nanny Belinda is amazing, and it's actually easier for her when Wyatt has a friend over."

"Tell me about it." I finally understood why parents made such a big deal about playdates, especially for only children. I loved them because it meant I didn't have to play cars or hide and seek or whatever for an hour or two.

Inside, I inhaled deeply once again. The air was musty and the light dim, but I could smell the long stories of this house. And when I looked around, the 12-foot ceilings in the central hall met the saffron-colored plaster walls with the loveliest crown molding I'd ever seen. It was scalloped and beveled in an intricate pattern that added a touch of elegance to the otherwise simple lines of the room.

"If you all will follow me, I'll introduce you to my husband, Mark." She led us down the hall into what was clearly an addition at the back of the house, where a sunny modern kitchen extended out to the edge of a bluff overlooking what had to be the Rose River.

I sighed and said, "This is beautiful. Wow. Thank you so much for having us out, Ms., Um...."

"I'm so sorry," our host said. "I totally neglected to introduce myself. I'm Mariah Owen." She turned to a thin, smiling man at the table by the windows. "And this is my husband, Mark. Mark, this is Paisley. You know Saul, and this little man is Sawyer."

"It's nice to meet all of you. Can I get you some coffee?" Mark said as he stood. "Sawyer, would you like some hot chocolate?"

I felt Sawyer nod against my thighs. "He would, but he prefers 'warm' chocolate," I said.

"You got it. Please have a seat." He pointed toward the large round table he had just left.

The three of us sat down, Sawyer settled on my lap, and Mark brought over a glass coffee carafe and mugs. Then, he popped another mug into the microwave for fifteen seconds and carried over a perfectly lukewarm cup of hot cocoa for my son, who proceeded to drink it in three seconds flat and then say, "Can I go play with Wyatt now?"

"He warms up quick," I said with a smile.

"Sure thing, Sawyer." Mariah said as she put out a hand. "Come with me, and I'll introduce you to Wyatt and Belinda. I think they're in the sandbox."

Without another glance at me, my son walked out the door off the kitchen toward what I could now see was a very large sandbox with not just one but two kid-sized excavators in it. "I may never get him to leave," I said to Saul.

Mark laughed. "That's what Wyatt's mother says. He stays with us a few days every month while she's getting treatments. Gives both of them a break."

"Oh no, cancer," I said.

"Yeah, ovarian. The chemo seems to be working, though, so I'm hopeful for my baby sis," Mark said and then cleared his throat.

"She'll be in our prayers," Saul said. "Do they live close?"

"Richmond. She's got a great team of doctors, and her husband is amazing. But it's hard for everyone when she's so sick. This way, I get to be close to my nephew, and they get to rest and recover without worrying about him." Mark sighed. "It's a big silver lining for a really hard time."

I nodded. "I'm glad you guys can be together, and thanks for letting Sawyer play. He loves making friends."

"Anytime he wants to come over, just give us a call." Mark laughed. "But if you agree to help us out, you might just be here yourself for a while."

"Tell me more about what you're looking for." I knew what Saul had said, of course, and I was already sold on the idea. But I wanted to hear from the homeowners exactly what they wanted me to do and on what terms. It gave me a chance to commit for myself and not put Saul in the middle.

Mariah walked back in and sat down beside me before pouring herself a cup of coffee. "What are we talking about?"

"I was just about to tell Paisley about the project and scope of work," Mark said.

"You're so formal, dear," she said with a smile and a soft squeeze of his hand. "Mark works in grants, so he's always talking in business terms." She winked at her husband. "Go right ahead."

"Well, the gist of it is this – every nook and cranny in this house is full of stuff. I don't think anyone who has lived here has ever donated, sold, or thrown away anything." Mark sighed. "We don't even know where to begin because we can't tell what's trash and what's treasure."

"Basically, we'd like to bring you on as a contractor, of sorts, to oversee the sorting of the things in the house. I expect you can handle most of it on your own, but we are happy to pay for experts on particular items if need be," Mariah added.

"Wow. Okay. I'd love to do that. Do you have a timeframe in mind?" I asked.

"As soon as possible, but we want the job done well. We really don't want to toss something that is valuable in any way. We'd rather someone who can use it get it," Mariah said. "And we want you to take anything you can sell, of course."

I smiled. "I like the sound of that, but before I give you my formal answer, do you mind if we look around?"

"Absolutely," Mariah said. "But just one more bit of business, what is your hourly fee?"

I stared at her for a long second and then looked over at Saul, who just shrugged.

"My hourly fee? I'm sorry. I think I'm not quite understanding. I thought my payment was to simply take any of the materials I could sell." Either option was appealing, but I did want to be clear on the terms.

Mark laughed. "You think we'd ask you to do a job this big on the off chance there is something worth money in here? No, we believe in paying people for their hard work." He sat forward. "To be clear, you are welcome to anything you find that is worth taking, and we will pay you your hourly fee for your work, including sorting and supervising."

I took another deep breath. "Well, in that case, I'd still like to look around if I may, but I'd also like to say yes."

Mariah slapped her hand on the table. "Excellent. Oh, but I should say that we do want to hear about what you find just because we're very curious."

"Of course," I said. "I'll probably be running around with things to show you all the time."

"Excellent," Mark said. "I'll draw up a contract this afternoon and get it over to you for signature. I do need to know that hourly rate, though." He winked at me.

I froze. I had never worked for an hourly rate before, and I had no idea what to charge.

"Her usual rate is \$100 an hour," Saul said matter-of-factly.

I looked over at him, my mouth hanging open, but before I could say something about "giving a discount" or "a special exception" so as to save Saul's reputation and assuage my own guilt, Mark said, "Great. I'll have the paperwork over later today."

At some point, I was going to get used to the fact that people paid well for hard work when they were well-paid for their own work. But I wasn't used to it yet, so as we stood to tour the house, I felt a little floaty, like I was gliding instead of walking. I decided I could adjust to that feeling.

The house was majestic and beautiful in the way that old plantation houses often are. It wasn't what I'd call cozy, but it was striking. As we walked through parlors and sitting rooms, all with fireplaces and fireplace screens designed to keep the direct heat off the delicate ankles of the women while they sewed, I pictured myself in a large skirt with my embroidery hoop in hand stitching flowers for hours at night because I had nothing else to do. Somehow, that didn't appeal as much as I thought it might.

The back rooms of the house – the dining room and the library – were open to the view out the back with floor-to-ceiling windows that were gorgeous but would have meant it was a challenge to keep the rooms warm in the winter.

Upstairs, the central hallway was lined with bedrooms, each with a view of the surrounding landscape that was simply gorgeous. I could almost picture sheep grazing in the front pastures, and I imagined that in the winter, the river was visible through the trees that lined it. People in that time period surely knew how to set a house.

"Your house is beautiful," I told Mark and Mariah.

Mariah nodded. "She is. A bit stark, and we hope to update

her a bit. Make her a bit more homey, but we're going to preserve the architectural integrity. Maybe just brighten the paint a bit, add some extra heat and AC," she said as she waved her hand in front of her face. It was a bit warm on the second floor.

I looked around the bedroom in which we stood for another minute, trying my best to be polite and not lunge toward the wardrobe in the corner to see what delights it held.

My anticipation must have shown because Mark smiled at me and said, "You're dying to see what's in there, aren't you?" He tilted his head to the mahogany cabinet that stretched from floor to ceiling.

I nodded and resisted the urge to clap my hands with delight. "Definitely. Do you mind?"

"That's why you're here," Mariah said.

I pranced over to the wardrobe and slowly opened the door, not sure what I'd find. Inside, instead of clothes hanging, as one might expect, I found stacks of bankers' boxes. Carefully, I lifted the top one off the shelf, surprised by how heavy it was, and set it down at my feet. Then, I sat on the floor, cross-legged, and opened the box.

Inside, I saw groups of letters bound together with twine, some loose sheets of paper, and several leather-bound books. I could hardly wait to look at all of it, but I picked up one of the books first. When I opened the first page, I smiled. "It's a ledger for the plantation, expenses and income." I turned the book to show it to everyone and looked up expecting to see the delight in their faces.

Instead, I was greeted by blank stares and remembered that most people didn't find columns of numbers in faded hand-writing to be as exciting as I did. I nodded. "This will tell us a lot about the workings of the plantation. Where they bought what, who they did business with, and even - if we're lucky - some of what the enslaved people here did with their time."

Mariah nodded, and while she was now smiling, I could tell she still wasn't convinced that even that information was important. "For people descended from enslaved people, these kinds of ledgers often give the only information they have about their ancestors. In that way, and in others, these books are invaluable." I gently closed the book and then stood up.

"If I may," I said as I walked back over to them, "could I ask if you would mind donating these records to the Octonia Historical Society? I don't have use for them personally, but I know Xzanthia Nicholas at the Society would love to have them."

"That's a wonderful idea," Mark said. "We can box them up and take them over later today if you'd like."

I appreciated his enthusiasm, but I needed to slow his roll just a bit. "Actually, it might be helpful for Ms. Nicholas to see the items as they are now. They might be grouped together by date or some other method." I looked from Mark to Mariah, and they seemed to understand. "Would you mind if I invited her out with me tomorrow to sort these items? Then, she and I could take them to the Historical Society for you when we're done."

"A lovely idea," Mariah said. "We'll have coffee and scones ready at 9."

I smiled. "Wonderful. I assume you have other things you'd like me to sort, too?" I asked with a growing sense that this might just be the project I've been waiting for, in more ways than one. At that moment, I couldn't have told you why, but I definitely felt this opportunity was going to yield something big.

For the next half-hour, we walked from room to room, opening wardrobes and closets, digging through drawers, and even venturing into the attic and outbuildings to get a peek at what was there. The only building we didn't visit that Mark and Mariah wanted me to salvage from was the barn, and the only reason we didn't go there was because I was too overwhelmed by what I'd already seen to even begin to take in another space.

It looked like I was going to have a couple of months of work ahead of me, and I couldn't wait to get started. "Thank you so much for this opportunity," I said as I shook the Owens' hands. "I'll see you in the morning."

Just then, Sawyer came charging around the house with a tiny boy close behind him. "You can't catch me. Nana nana boo boo," he taunted.

Wyatt then lunged and tackled him, and while I held my breath to see if anyone was hurt or mad, they stood up and laughed. "You got me," Saw said with a grin. "You're so fast."

I heard my own voice in his words and smiled. "Time to go, Sawyer. Maybe you can come play again soon."

He sprinted toward us before turning to wave goodbye to his new friend. "See you soon, Wyatt," he said.

As the three of us walked to our vehicles, I was grinning ear to ear, both because of the job and my son's new friend.

"Going to be a good gig, Paisley girl?" Saul asked.

"Going to be the best," I said. I could feel it.

2

———————

That night at dinner, as Santiago cooked us an amazing lemon-thyme chicken that made even the kale salad underneath it appealing, I told him about our time at the Sumner Place with the Owens and then filled him in on what Saul had told me on the way home.

"So apparently, they made their money selling hemp for fabric," I said still surprised and delighted that such a thing was possible. I had been a big hemp necklace wearer in my younger years, and now I loved the hemp and cotton t-shirts Santi had gotten me for my birthday because they didn't get the little holes at the belly that all my other shirts did. They were durable and comfy. "I'm wondering who they grow for."

"Is that what they're going to do at the Sumner Place? Grow hemp?" Santi asked, and I could hear a little edge to his voice.

"I know you know this, but hemp and marijuana aren't the same thing. Are you worried about that?" I asked, trying to figure out what was making him a bit nervous.

"No, actually, I'm not bothered at all if they want to grow pot, as long as they have the proper permits and such. It's legal now, and that's just fine with me." He moved the skillet off the burner and turned to me. "My issue is that a lot of other people don't know the difference. If they're growing out there, I probably need to talk to them to be sure we're supporting their security measures."

I nodded. "That makes sense. Want to go with Ms. Nicholas and me in the morning? I can text Mariah to let her know you're coming."

Santi plated the chicken over the greens and then slid fresh-roasted brussels sprouts onto the plate. "Sure. Thanks." He stepped to the door and called Sawyer in from where he was digging a rather massive hole in the side yard. "Dinner, Saw."

My son dropped his blue shovel and sprinted to the door. "Did you cook?" he asked Santi as he slid into his chair across from me.

I turned away and rolled my eyes at my fiancé. These days, Sawyer almost never ate what I made, even when I catered to his preschooler's palate with macaroni and cheese and chicken nuggets. But whenever Santi cooked, which was most nights now, Saw was ready and willing to try-- and usually consume -- most anything, even roasted brussels sprouts.

Tonight, he waited, as I had taught him, until Santiago sat down beside me, and then he dug in, starting with the kale. I shook my head and laughed as I took my own bite and groaned. It was delicious.

"Sawyer, did you have fun playing at the big house today?" I asked between bites.

My son nodded as he chewed and then said, "It was so fun. They had a *huge* slide."

"Oh really," Santi said. "A huge one, huh? How huge?"

"This big," Saw said as he spread his arms as wide as they would go. "I kept landing on my butt."

I laughed. "Ooh, did that hurt?"

"Nope, I've got cushions." Saw said as he patted his behind.

"Yes, yes you do," I said. "You and Wyatt had a lot of fun. Do you want to go back with me tomorrow?"

Saw wiggled in his chair and nodded. "Wyatt said we can go down to the river if I bring my swim stuff."

"Great. I'll double-check to be sure that's okay, and we can all go in the morning," I looked over at Santi and winked. "It'll be a family outing."

Santi squeezed my knee under the table. We were still a couple months out from our wedding, but since Santiago had moved in, it felt like we were already coming together as a family. After all, only Santi could get this boy to eat kale and brussels sprouts in one meal.

THE NEXT MORNING, with Mariah's enthusiastic support, the three of us made our way to the Sumner Place. When we pulled up, Xzanthia Nicholas, the director of the historical society, was just stepping out of her car. She stood to her full height, took a deep breath, and said, "A perfect Virginia summer day."

I shook my head as I walked toward her. "If what you mean by perfect is 'stinking hot,' then I agree." I was already turning red from head to toe. "I can't believe you like this heat."

She smiled at me as we walked toward the front door of the big brick house. "I can't believe you don't."

When I had called the day before to tell her about the trove of papers the Owenses had in their wardrobe, she had calmly replied, "Did you, by chance, ask if they would be comfortable with me seeing said papers?"

I had smiled and laughed. The calmer Ms. Nicholas became, the more excited she was. It was a trait of her personality that I loved, especially since I was the opposite. Excitement made me childlike. It made her dignified.

When I had told her that they welcomed us the next morning, she said, "What time?" and "I'll bring archival folders and boxes."

Now, here we were, Santiago, Sawyer, Ms. Nicholas, and I loaded down with folders and collapsed boxes, ready to work. Fortunately, Mariah and Mark met us at the door and took Sawyer's load because as soon as Wyatt rounded the corner, my son was off with nary a wave in our direction. "Oh, man, he's excited," I said. "Is Belinda okay with this?"

"Are you kidding?" Mariah said. "She gets to sit and read instead of build roads in the sand. She's delighted."

I laughed and nodded. I knew that feeling far too well. "Well, we're pretty delighted, too. Mariah Owen, this is Xzanthia Nicholas, director of the Octonia Historical Society."

The women exchanged pleasantries, then Mark said to Santi, "Let's go talk about the plans we have, Sheriff, make sure we're helping you keep us safe."

Santi squeezed my arm and then followed Mark into the dining room while Mariah led Ms. Nicholas and me directly to the room with the wardrobe. I appreciated that she didn't feel the compulsion that many of us Southern women have to make small talk and spend time in pleasantries. All three of us were about business.

When we walked into the bedroom, I saw that a small table had been set up in the corner with a coffee carafe, cream and sugar, and a glass-covered plate filled with what looked like some of the best scones I had ever seen. It took an immense amount of willpower for me not to put down my supplies and go right to the table, but I followed Ms. Nicholas's lead and moved toward the wardrobe instead.

Fortunately, Ms. Nicholas had done this kind of work many times before, and she had a system she had already explained to me. As she began to open archival boxes and set out a variety of pencils and one pen on the floor between the window and the wardrobe, I could see I was in good hands with this work today.

"Would you care to join us, Ms. Owen?" Ms. Nicholas asked our host. "We could always use another set of hands and eyes."

Mariah grinned. "I didn't want to impose, but I have to admit I am so curious. If you don't mind...."

"Please," Ms. Nicholas gestured to a portion of the floor across from where she had just gracefully folded down to sit, and Mariah joined her. I, with slightly less poise and a small grunt, got myself folded down to the floor, too. Without further ado, Ms. Nicholas explained her process for sorting archival materials.

"We move box by box first, making note," she handed us each a pencil and a yellow legal pad, "of the contents in each box – type of document, date, and any prominent names that are easy to spot."

Mariah and I nodded as Ms. Nicholas continued, "Then, once we know what is in each box, we can decide if the organizational strategy with which these items were stored was simply one of efficiency or actual content."

I smiled and was grateful I had suggested we bring in Ms. Nicholas today because, as I had expected, she had a definite plan here.

With her plan set forth, Ms. Nicholas stood, removed a box for each of us from the wardrobe and set us to work. The box I had in front of me now was entirely full of letters tied into stacks with a twine much like the one Sawyer and I used to stake up our peas in the garden. With Ms. Nicholas's permission, I snipped the twine and reviewed each set of letters. Each set was indeed organized by sender, and so I wrote down how many envelopes were in each set, from whom the letter was sent, and who received it. Most were notes to women in the Sumner family, and while I didn't know the family well enough to recognize the women by name, I guessed that the letters I was seeing were written by younger people, given the bubbly shape of the handwriting. Loops seemed a sort of universal element of young women's handwriting, no matter the time period.

After I made my way through about half of my box, I excused myself to use the restroom and then came back to work only after sipping a cup of coffee and consuming – far away from the old papers – what truly was one of the most amazing blueberry scones I had ever eaten.

When I settled back down on the floor, Ms. Nicholas took her leave and did the same as I did, except with the poise of a supermodel. When she came back, the three of us finished up our boxes at roughly the same time. "Care to tell us briefly what you found?" Ms. Nicholas asked as she put her materials back in her box and closed the lid.

I shared about the letters I had viewed and placed back in my own box, and Mariah said she had mostly business papers including the ledger I had shown her the day before, as well as a couple of smaller farm books that detailed the planting and harvest schedules for the plantation.

Ms. Nicholas said her box was full of similar items: letters, ledgers, and other miscellany including some papers that looked to be shopping lists. "Most interesting," she said as she held her bejeweled fingers against her chestnut-colored cheek. Even when she was pondering, she was elegant. "Shall we move along?"

For the next two hours, the three of us perused boxes and made notes. Most of what I looked at was correspondence, and while I had encountered some letters of a sort that had been really crucial in previous research of mine, the majority were the usual small talk or family discussions that, while precious, were not of truly important historic merit.

I gathered from Mariah's infrequent sighs and smiles that she was enjoying what she was reading but not being monumentally bowled over by it. Of course, I couldn't be sure of that since she might have been a fairly reserved woman, but somehow, I figured she might be a bit like me, unable to keep good news to herself.

Ms. Nicholas was another story altogether. She might have unearthed a signed original copy of the Declaration of Independence and continued in her methodical, careful way through the rest of the box before she shared her find as being of potential merit. Still, she seemed to be taking a fair number of notes, and I hoped she was encountering some great stories at least.

Mariah finished her box first and stood up to stretch and refresh the coffee carafe. I was done next and began to tidy up our notes. Finally, Ms. Nicholas finished, stood, stretched, and when Mariah handed her a full mug of coffee, Ms. Nicholas said, "Well, I do believe we have a real discovery here."

Her tone was so matter-of-fact that I thought I might have misunderstood, so I said, "What do you mean by 'discovery,' Ms. Nicholas?"

She gestured to the box she had just perused. "Well, if I am right, Mrs. Sumner was suffering from postpartum depression and killed her husband."

I stared at the historical society director and then looked over at Mariah, who was standing with her mouth open and a coffee mug halfway to it. "Come again," she finally said.

"I can't be sure without further corroboration of course, but I do believe that Eliza Sumner was a murderer." Ms. Nicholas nodded for emphasis. "Perhaps you'd like to take a look at the evidence."

"Evidence of what?" Santiago said from the doorway. "You women doing police work in here?"

I shook my head. "Not yet," I said, "but it may well be that. Please show us the journal, Ms. Nicholas."

"Indeed." She took two brief steps to the box she had just

finished reviewing, lifted out a small, suede-bound book, and said, "The most clear evidence is from May 1871 until June of that same year."

Mariah gestured toward the door. "If it won't do any harm, Ms. Nicholas, maybe we could go to the dining room and sit more comfortably."

I was grateful for the suggestion since my lower back was ready for the support of a chair after all that floor time.

"Of course," Ms. Nicholas said. "I'll bring the box so we can pull additional of her journals if needed." She looked at me. "Your notes might help, too?" She smiled at me, and I picked up the legal pads from the floor, not sure if Ms. Nicholas's tone was friendly or school-marmish. Maybe a bit of both.

At the table, Mark joined us, and Ms. Nicholas informed him and Santi of what she felt fairly certain was a murder confession in the journal. Mark looked at her and said, "Does she outright say that?"

"No," Ms. Nicholas shook her head. "She doesn't, but she does discuss the ways one might disguise the flavor of mountain laurel in food."

"Wait," I said, "Mountain laurel is poisonous?"

"Very," Mark said. "It's beautiful, but if you're raising any kind of animals, like goats, you can't have it near them. It can kill them quickly, and humans too, as I understand it."

Mariah nodded. "That's right. I remember the extension agent telling us that if we were going to pasture goats near the woods we'd have to cut all the mountain laurel out." She sighed. "We decided to forgo the goats."

"Apparently, Mrs. Sumner knew it was poisonous," Santi said as he scanned the pages of the journal now in front of him. "She had some rather elaborate ways of slipping it into food for consumption."

"My favorite was plum pudding," Ms. Nicholas said with a

wink at me. My friend wasn't usually the playful sort, but I could see she was putting Santi on a bit.

Santi shook his head. "I see why this would be disturbing, but did you see anything else that indicated she might have actually poisoned anyone? Particularly her husband?"

"Keep reading," Ms. Nicholas said and then looked down at her notes. "The entries for the third and fourth of June will be of particular interest, I believe."

Santi turned a few pages, picked the book up and held it so his shadow didn't fall across the faint handwriting. Then, he began to read out loud:

My dear husband has fallen deathly ill after dinner tonight. It appears that our machinations have been successful. Yet, had I known he would groan so, a more expeditious means might have been chosen, perhaps a broken neck from a fall off his favorite horse. But there is nothing to be done for that. We must all simply endure until he no longer does so.

I LET OUT my own far less painful groan. "Well, that does sound remarkably like a confession," I said.

Santi turned the page and read again:

The night was arduous but just before dawn the haunting sounds of his cries ended, and I felt as if the angels themselves were singing. I know that is not true. We shall suffer for what we have done, but for now, we have peace. All of us. Each of us. Peace again.

"SHE DOESN'T SOUND contrite at all," Mariah said. "Wait, Ms. Nicholas, you said something earlier about postpartum depression. What do you mean?"

. . .

"WELL, I am expert neither by training or experience, but it seems to me that Mrs. Sumner was feeling quite, shall we say, down after the birth of each of her children," Ms. Nicholas said. "In many of her journal entries, she talks about her deep sadness and about how she doesn't know if she will be able to survive another day."

"THAT DOES SOUND like my experience of postpartum depression," I said, not really wanting to elaborate further.

MARIAH SHOOK HER HEAD. "You mean like that woman who drove the car with her children into the lake? That was terrible!"

I SIGHED. "It was terrible, but also probably preventable. We are not good as a society at dealing with women's mental health."

"Are you thinking that her illness had something to do with her husband's death?" Santi asked as he studied Ms. Nicholas's face. "Do you think she might have killed him because of her depression?"

Ms. Nicholas shook her head. "I don't know, Sheriff. But it might be worth exploring that question. That is, if you're going to investigate this murder." She bowed her head gently.

I looked at the faces of every person in the room and wondered if I was ever going to get a salvage job that didn't involve a murder investigation. At this point, I doubted it.

SANTI BEGAN TAKING notes on the journals. Ms. Nicholas continued to sort the papers. I decided to see what Sawyer was up to. I needed a little break from the darker parts of history.

When I asked Mark where I might find the boys, he said they had gone down to the river, and I decided to look forward to the walk across the fields.

THE DAY WAS HOT, but a little less humid than usual and there was a breeze coming up off the water that made it almost pleasant to stroll. I watched the clusters of no-see-ums flying through the air and studied them. There were bobbing patterns of sparrows under the brush along the roadbed, and I forced myself to take deep breaths. At least this murder wasn't recent. At least I hadn't discovered a body this time.

WHEN I REACHED the bank above the water, I could hear the boys' laughter, and when I looked down, my son was ardently splashing his friend in the face with river water. For his part, Wyatt was laughing with glee and Belinda was standing by, ankle deep in the water, a smile on her face too. The scene was quintessential summer.

I decided to keep my presence to myself for a little while and sat down on the riverbank, slightly obscured by a tree. There I could see Saw laugh and splash and run around in the shallow water without interrupting.

IT HAD TAKEN a couple years before I could really feel the joy of his childhood. While I had loved that boy from the moment I held him just after he was born, the struggle of my pregnancy and his birth had left me in some shadowy places for a while. I still had enjoyed his first laugh and watching him cruise around the house on his hands and knees. But the sharpness of those experiences just wasn't there. That's what postpartum depression had done to me, sort of dulled my experience of my son's infancy.

But now? I saw his joy and felt my own with the crispness I'd hoped to feel. They felt more real and powerful than anything else I'd experienced. Seeing him laugh and fall and gallop through the water without any sense of the hard things in the world was one of the most beautiful experiences of my life, and I was profoundly grateful for it.

After a few minutes, I decided to walk down the rest of the way to the water and dip my own feet in. I knew this was going to mean that I would be soaking wet shortly, but the heat of the day was catching up with me, and I decided that would be fun too. So for the next little bit, I splashed the boys and tried to protect Belinda from their games while she took a break on the shore. But of course, by the time we were done, all of us were soaked through, and all of us were laughing.

It was time for lunch, so I helped Belinda corral the boys up the hill and back to the house, where sandwiches and chips and those crazy juice bottles with animal faces were ready. I gave Saw a kiss on his forehead and went back upstairs, drying my hair with a towel Belinda had gotten me from the bathroom.

When I returned to the bedroom, Santi was carrying the last of the paper boxes out of the room to his car, and Ms. Nicholas was making a final inventory list of what she had collected for Mark and Mariah. "I'll formalize this after I review the material an additional time," she said. "But I don't want to take the material without leaving you some sort of written record of what you donated."

"ALL DONE." I asked. "Did you find anything new?"

MS. NICHOLAS SHOOK HER HEAD. "Not as far as I could see. But the sheriff did make some notes for his own purposes."

I NODDED. "Well, with the paperwork handled, how do you feel about me continuing on in other levels of research?" I turned to Mark and Mariah again.

"FINE WITH ME," Mark said, "but can I treat everyone to lunch first?"

I HADN'T WANTED to admit how hungry I was, especially after my swim in the river. But the mention of lunch made my stomach growl audibly. I blushed. "I guess you know my answer."

MARK SMILED. "Come on down to the kitchen. And I'll whip us up some salads. I think there's still half of the tiramisu I made yesterday in the fridge, too."

NO ONE HAD to suggest tiramisu to me twice, and I led the way down the stairs.

3

———————

Over lunch, we talked about what each of us knew of the Sumner family. I had gone to school with some of the descendants. And Ms. Nicholas had done a fair amount of research about this prominent family for the Historical Society. But when we really started to examine what we knew, it turned out most of our information was pretty general. More like oral history than historical fact. Now, I was never one to discount oral history as valid and useful, but it came with the mystery. That seemed odd for a family as prominent as the Sumners. Even the most withdrawn and quiet wealthy white family in this area typically had a fairly extensively documented history available. That was just the nature of running a plantation. When you had that many people to do your work for you, you had plenty of time to write letters, record information, and keep ledgers. Basically, wealth gave you the privilege of recording your own history, as Ms. Nicholas said.

But in the case of the Sumners, this history was light. Scant, even... until today. It seemed nothing personal had ever really been shared about the family. I'd heard the Sumner kids talk about this big house in show-and-tell sometimes. The house had been part of garden tours in the late twentieth century. But we didn't have the sort of storied familiarity with the Sumner family that we did with other families from Octonia. It's kind of odd now that I thought about it.

"Maybe they were just a private family," Santi suggested.

I considered that. "Or maybe we just haven't had any real information about them because it's been tucked away in closets all these years."

"Maybe both." Ms. Nicholas said. "It might be useful to consider that none of these papers have ever been seen publicly before."

She had a point. "You think they were hiding something?"

Ms. Nicholas shrugged. "Some people's secrets are other people's gold mines." Upon imparting that bit of wisdom, Ms. Nicholas stood and thanked our hosts for the opportunity. Then she excused herself and left.

Mariah turned to me once Ms. Nicholas was gone and said, "she's quite a woman."

I laughed. "That she is."

After we all helped with lunch clean up, Mariah led me up to the attic and suggested I work my way down. "You'll need this though." She handed me a paper surgical mask. "The dust could kill you."

Something about that phrasing set my nerves a little on edge, but I forced a smile onto my face and said "Thanks" before making my way to the furthest, darkest corner. It had always been my life philosophy to start with the hardest thing and work to the easiest. The hardest thing up here seemed like that corner.

Most of the boxes were full of what all of us keep in our attics: Christmas decorations and photo albums full of images of people we're probably related to but don't know how. There were a couple of really great boxes of vintage clothes that I tugged over to the opening of the attic because they would be great to sell in the shop. I found a steamer trunk full of shampoo samples that spanned several decades and decided that might be worth keeping not only for the trunk, but for the Instagram photo opportunities with the packaging.

But it was the standing wardrobe in the high eaves near the center of the house that most fascinated me. Maybe because of what we'd found in the other wardrobe a floor below, or maybe it was my continuing fascination with Narnia. But the whole time I worked my way forward, I kept my eye on that piece of furniture. It was going to be my reward for all this dust and hard work.

By 3:30, I had made it through most of one side of the attic. I knew that Sawyer, as much fun as he was having, was going to be ready to go home soon. So I treated myself to opening the wardrobe.

I wasn't disappointed. Inside were two perfectly intact Confederate soldier uniforms. The gray wool smelled of body odor and dust. And when I carefully lifted each hanger off the wooden dowel in the middle of the cabinet, I could see that these were uniforms that had been worn, not just collected. Sweat stains under the armpits were still visible, and there was a rip in the arm of one of the jackets. These were treasures.

They were also worth a lot of money. And while I knew I could hold Mark and Mariah to the terms of our agreement and keep these for myself, I didn't feel like that was the ethical thing to do. I promised myself I would tell them about the uniforms as soon as I finished going through the rest of the wardrobe. And I hoped that they would still let me keep them. Because this kind of find could put a real dent in Sawyer's college fund.

The right-hand side of the wardrobe had six small drawers in it. I tried to imagine the kinds of clothing a man would keep in these drawers. Stockings. Garters. Did men wear garters?

Wigs. Could there be powdered wigs in here? I clearly had no knowledge of historical clothing.

But it turned out I didn't need that knowledge, because the drawers were full of what I think of as the tiny things of life. There were cufflinks and a couple of medals that looked like they could have come from some sort of military service. 2 shoehorns. A variety of cravats, I think would be the term we call them. And bow ties. All of it was fascinating.

The bottom drawer, though, held what most intrigued me: stacks of loose photographs. Some of them were tintypes. And given that a couple of the men in those were in gray uniforms, I figured they might be family photos of the people who wore the uniforms. Some were much more recent, probably from the 1940s or 50s with the deckle edges -- family snapshots of picnics and birthday parties. But it was the ones that were sepia toned, not daguerreotypes, but similar, that fascinated me the most because they were all portraits of children. As best I could tell, they weren't the same children over and over again, even though there were dozens of these pictures.

In some of the images little girls had ringlets that hung to their shoulders and fancy lace collars from what I imagined was the Victorian era. And in others, children were in knickers and what we would now call tank tops, and appeared to be posed as if they were playing. In others, infants were resting, sleeping quietly in their cradles, tiny bonnets over their heads. All of them were beautiful. And all of them were creepy.

I couldn't begin to figure out why I found the images creepy. Maybe it was because the children looked so posed or stiff in ways that Sawyer would never look. Or maybe it was the sort of blank expression in the children's eyes. I still wasn't sure, but I set the photos aside after flipping through them quickly because they gave me goosebumps.

I carefully gathered all the items from the wardrobe, including the uniforms, into an empty basket I found on the other side of the attic and carried it down the stairs. I was going to need help getting the bigger things down, but I wanted to talk to Mark and Mariah about these things first.

I found my hosts in the dining room with tumblers of whiskey and snack plates in front of them. And suddenly my stomach did its annoying thing of rumbling so loudly that Mark started to laugh.

"Join us, Paisley?" Mark asked. "The boys have just gone to town with Belinda to get ice cream. And we are enjoying the peace and quiet."

"That obvious, huh?" I said as I set my armful of treasures down on the table.

Mariah laughed. "Well, you have been working hard," she said as she stood and got me a glass of my own drink and a small plate. "Did you find anything?"

I took a deep breath. "I did." I carefully unfolded the two uniforms and laid them across the table. These," I said, "you will want to keep. They are incredibly valuable, I expect."

Mark shook his head. "That's great, Paisley, but they are yours by the terms of our agreement. I'm glad to get to see them though." He studied the fabric. "Confederate."

I nodded. "Definitely. Are you sure you don't want to keep them?"

Mariah shook her head. "No, you keep them. We don't have the time to do the research to sell them properly anyway and we made commitments to you. We will honor that"

I smiled. "Is it bad to say I hoped you were going to say that?"

Mark and Mariah laughed. "No, not at all," Mariah said. "What else did you find?"

I laid out the other things I'd found in the wardrobe and explained that I would need to do research to understand more about what each of the things was. But then I pulled aside the top photos from the twentieth century and spread out the images of the children.

Mariah gasped. "These are memorial photos." she said quietly.

I studied her face, then admitted, "I'm sorry, I don't know what memorial photos are."

She carefully lifted an image close to her face and ran a soft finger over the child's cheek. "They're photos that were taken of people, especially children, after they died." she sighed. "It was a tender thing to do at the time. But now? They're pretty terrifying. Just because of our cultural practices around death."

I looked from her to Mark.

Mark said, "Mariah has been interested in memorial photos for a long time."

I waited for him to say more, but he didn't. And I looked back at Mariah.

She said, "My grandmother had a picture of her little brother who died in infancy. When I was about eight, I found that picture in her drawer and asked about it. My grandmother always told me the truth, so she explained what it was. It didn't scare me then. They still don't scare me now. But I do feel a lot of sadness when I see them. So many children died so early."

I swallowed hard. "Maybe you would like to keep these?"

Mariah looked up at me then. "If you don't mind, I would, but just for a little while. I have studied these so intensively. I can date them by the clothing and the posing pretty easily. Maybe that would help tell more of the Sumner story."

I nodded. "Sounds like a great idea." But then I frowned. "I know infant mortality rates used to be a lot higher, but this is a lot of photos for one family. Maybe you can figure out the story behind that."

Mariah nodded. "It's a good point. I can try."

I took the last sip of my whiskey and relished the warmth that spread all the way to my feet. It was nice to have friends to enjoy a drink and talk with. "I did find a few more things in the attic but I'll need some help carrying them down," I said.

"Did you mark them in some way?" Mark asked. "If so, I can bring them down for you this evening."

I shook my head. "Some of them are too heavy. Santi and I can get them tomorrow, if that's OK with you." I glanced around. "Unless he's still here by chance."

Mark shook his head. "I'm sorry. He asked me to tell you he'd be back at 4:30. He was going to go into town and to begin looking at the information we found earlier."

I looked down at my watch. 4:25. "Well, he and I can get them now if that's okay with you, get them out of your way"

Mariah said, "No need. You can get them tomorrow. They're not in our way at this point." She smiled and looked over my shoulder. "Besides, I think you're going to be quite busy in just a second."

I turned to look behind me and saw my son running full tilt toward the house, his face covered in chocolate from chin to eyebrows. I laughed. "I think you may be right."

I intercepted my son at the front door, before he could spread chocolate all over the furniture, and told him we'd wait outside for Santi. I had the uniforms and the other miscellaneous stuff from the wardrobe in my arms. I figured I could spend the evening researching and pricing those materials. The uniforms, of course, would have to go to a specialty auction. But I had a friend in Charlottesville who might be able to help me with that.

While we waited, Mark and Mariah, Wyatt, Belinda, and Sawyer played a game of freeze tag in the yard. I enjoyed watching them and was pleased again by the way friendship filled life up so much.

. . .

AS SOON AS Sawyer was in bed that night I called Ms. Nicholas and let her know what I had found in the wardrobe and the other miscellaneous items I'd located in the trunk aside from the photos, which I knew the Historical Society would treasure because they loved photos. I didn't yet know what I was doing with the other materials. Part of me really wanted to be generous and donate the uniforms for their museum.

But I knew that Ms. Nicholas would probably refuse them for two reasons. First, they were Confederate uniforms. Neither one of us really wanted to perpetuate the strange, rather racist reverence people had for the Confederacy. Second, she knew even better than I that those uniforms were worth a lot of money. And that I needed money.

SURE ENOUGH, when I told her about the uniforms she gave me the name of a museum curator in Richmond who could authenticate and value them for me. And then she suggested a particular auction house who could bring top dollar for the pair once they were authenticated. "Glad you found them, Paisley" she said. "But they belong in a certain kind of museum with a certain kind of interpretation. I suspect you know what I mean?"

I did know what she meant. These uniforms should be in a museum that would responsibly and accurately discuss the Confederacy, not in some Southern heritage-claiming roadside stand that hawked Confederate flags and small statues of Robert E Lee. "Thank you for the recommendation, Ms. Nicholas" I said. "Once Mariah is done with the photos, I'll bring those to you for the collection."

"I will be grateful for the donation, Paisley." She hung up, and I opened my laptop. I had research to do.

Fortunately, Santi had his own research to complete. He was surrounded by stacks of paper, many quite old, from the looks of them. And I gathered from what he'd said at dinner that he had been to see Ms. Nicholas earlier himself and asked for her help in finding out whatever she could about the Sumner family. He was clearly taking this murder possibility quite seriously.

As I typed in various descriptions of the military medals I'd found, I asked him "Is this an intellectual search, a full investigation, or something else?" I looked up for my laptop to see him studying my face.

He smiled. "It's a murder investigation, Paisley. Even you know there's no statute of limitations on murder."

"I do know that," I said. "But I also know that whoever killed Mr. Sumner is long dead themselves. So my question still stands."

"Let's just say it's intellectual curiosity for the moment." He winked at me. There was something he wasn't saying, but he wasn't going to say it now.

For the next two hours, we both typed and flipped pages and talked about what we found. And by the end of the night, I had a valuation on the two World War One medals I'd found and a good sense that the gold cufflinks were worth a fair amount of cash. And there'd be a fun sewing project for Mika with the cravats and bow ties. She had been ecstatic when I said I'd give them to her.

As we got ready for bed though, I was still disconcerted by those photos of the children. I had looked up memorial photos, or mourning photos as they were sometimes called, and seen that just as Mariah said, they were really a trend; a sort of way of capturing the life of a child even after the child had died. Photos have been taken of famous people after death, and of adults too. But it seemed that pictures of children were one of the most popular, maybe because their lives have been so brief.

Aside from just finding the practice creepy – I could never imagine taking a photograph of Sawyer if he died – I was just stuck on the fact that there were so many photos of so many children in that wardrobe. I knew that once printing had evolved, people often made copies of these photos and distributed them, but these didn't look like copies. The images I had found in the wardrobe looked like actual photos. I didn't know how to make sense of that.

When we got into bed, I finally voiced my fear. "Santi, do you think it's possible that someone in that house killed all those children?"

Santi pulled me close to him and said, "I don't know, Paisley. I certainly hope not."

THE NEXT MORNING when I got to the Owens' house, Mariah was waiting for me. "I've just made muffins, and I wanted to tell you what I found out about the photographs," she said.

"Oh good, both of those things sound good. I didn't sleep very well last night trying to figure out where those pictures had come from." I followed her into the dining room where she poured me a large mug of coffee and handed me a very generously proportioned blueberry muffin with crystals of sugar on the top.

She pointed to a chair at the table as she poured her own coffee and then sat down with me before tearing off the top of her muffin and beginning to eat the bottom.

I looked at my new friend and said, "Please tell me you are going to eat the top of that muffin."

She grinned, and small wrinkles formed at the corners of her eyes. "Of course I am. I'm not a psychopath. I just save it for last."

I laughed. "Ah yes," I said "That's the same method I use on trail mix. At the end, it's just like eating a bag of chocolates." I took a bite of my own muffin. When I swallowed, I said "So tell me about the pictures. Stop these morbid thoughts I have going through my head."

She smiled. "I'm actually very glad I can do that because it was wearing on me too. As soon as you left yesterday, I started researching. Fortunately, it didn't take long for me to figure out why we have all those images?"

"Oh good. So tell me what you learned." I took that opportunity to both listen and enjoy more of my delicious muffin.

"I looked at the stamps on the back of some of the more recent photos and saw that they were all labeled as coming from one photographer down in Charlottesville." She pulled the stack of photos out from where they had been sitting on a chair beside her. "A little internet digging helped me learn that J.A. Karella was actually the grandson of the Sumners who built this house. He was the photographer for many of these images." She turned over one of the cards, and I saw the words *Karella Photo Studio, Charlottesville, VA.*

I let out a huge sigh. "So these were images he took as part of his profession. That's good. That's very good." I sighed again. "Still creepy, but good."

Mariah laughed. "Yeah, it really does take a while to get used to seeing these. Plus, there's more." She took a sip of her coffee. "According to Ms. Nicholas, the family had been doing portrait photographs for generations. They had been some of the first in the area to actually take photos. And so it wasn't just Mr. Karella but maybe his father and grandfather too."

"So that explains why there were so many from such a long period of time," I said. "Did they take other kinds of pictures, too, or just pictures of kids after they died?" I wasn't sure I wanted to hear the answer to my question, but I knew I needed to ask it.

"Oh, they were full service photographers, so they did weddings and funerals but also formal portraits for people, photos for the newspaper. Once I started looking into them, I saw the names *Karella* and *Sumner* everywhere."

She took her laptop and pulled it close in front of her before opening it. "I'm absolutely sure you're familiar with Newspapers.com, right? So you can take a look for yourself, but that's where I was able to find a lot more information. It's pretty interesting actually, especially since we didn't really know how they were making their money. The descendants had been sort of evasive about the family history when we bought the place."

"They were?" I asked. "That's interesting."

"Yeah. Mark and I only really realized they had been a bit cagey when we were talking about things last night. It was what you said about how we didn't really know much about them and that that was kind of weird. That made us remember that Solomon Sumner, who had sold us the house, had been very forthcoming with blueprints and construction plans and renovation details. But when we started to ask about the family history, saying that we wanted to try to preserve it and honor it, he basically cut us off."

From the doorway behind me, Mark added "At the time, I thought he was just in a hurry or didn't want to be friendly with the new buyers because it was painful to sell his family home. But now I'm wondering if there was something more. Basically, all he told us was that his family had owned the place for seven generations but now he couldn't afford to keep it up and he was ready to move on to new stories."

"Is that how he said it? New stories?" I asked.

"Yeah, that's exactly what he said. Even then, I thought that was a little weird, but he was a little eccentric, so I didn't really make much of it," Mark said.

I stood to pour myself another cup of coffee and said, "Eccentric how?"

Mark and Mariah both laughed. Mariah said, "Would you believe he wore a monocle and a top hat?"

"Like Mr. Peanut?" I said with a laugh.

"Exactly," Mark said. "He was really short too, so he looked even more like the character."

I chuckled and then sat back down with my fresh cup of coffee and made a decision to dig further into this interesting family. "Do you guys mind if I research more about the Sumners and write about it in my newsletter? I know you wanted some information for your own purposes, but would it be disruptive to you if I wrote about it more publicly? We might learn more."

Mariah shook her head. "No problem with that as far as I'm concerned." She studied my face a minute and then said, "Would you mind including a bit about the current owners?" She blushed. "Explain that we want to honor the family and would love any information people can provide?"

I smiled. 'I love that idea," I said. It would probably get the Owens more information, but it would also build a little good will with the community. "I'll copy you on the draft before I send it."

"No need," Mark said. "Just put us on your mailing list so we have a heads up when it goes out."

I looked from him to his wife and marveled inwardly about how much trust they had in me. It felt good.

4

Mark and I brought the boxes and trunks down from the attic and loaded them into the back of my Subaru. Then I climbed back up into the sweltering attic and began perusing the items in the other half of the space. I found a lot more holiday decorations, a couple of boxes of remarkably well-preserved old books, and more vintage clothes.

But it was the massive trunk full of photographs that was most exciting. Given what Mariah had told me about the family business, I was quick to determine that these were more of the photos that Karella and Sumner had taken at their studio, and I knew that everyone would be eager to see them. Fortunately, it looked like someone had already sorted out the funeral photos, and these seemed largely happy images – family groups and wedding portraits.

As I quickly filtered through the photos, I wondered about an idea I had for the historical society. I'd seen local organizations provide scanning and dating services for the photographs of local citizens, and I wondered if Ms. Nicholas might entertain an idea – with voluntary donations from guests – for the society. She'd be able to put some of these photos out and get some identification of folks and also provide services for the local families who had photos they wanted to preserve well.

I was mulling over this idea when I went to check out the last corner of the attic. There, I could just see what looked like a tiny pink suitcase, and I smiled with the hope that it might be full of vintage doll clothes, maybe even an old doll.

But when I opened the little rectangle by flipping open the brass latch, I saw not doll clothes but the clothes of a child: a faded pair of blue jeans, a t-shirt with a distinctly 1970s-style design, and two pairs of socks. There was also a slim pink book tucked into the back net pocket of the suitcase, and when I picked it up, the gold-embossed word *Diary* glimmered in the weak light from the window above me.

I sat down carefully on a rafter and opened the book. There, on the front page, was the name Lily Sumner, and what appeared to be her birthday, April 5, 1969. A child's drawing of a cat with big ears and a fluffy tail decorated the inside cover. When I turned to the first lined page, I saw it was filled with the formal cursive script of a girl who had not yet made her handwriting her own. Her Rs still had the two pointy tips, and each word was finished with a curled flourish. Most of us scrubbed off those formalities by middle school, so I guessed this book had belonged to someone a bit younger.

With the diary in hand, I scooted my butt along the rafter until I could sit back against the wall. Then, I began to read. The first few entries were typical pre-teen stuff. What she'd done that day, which seemed to occur in the middle of summer since there was no mention of school, and who she'd seen, girlfriends mostly. A couple times she mentioned boys she or her friends liked, but by and large, this young woman was writing about her daily life, using the diary for its original purpose.

But in early August, the entries began to change. The girl began talking about "him," a male she never named but given that she mentioned seeing him drive up in his car, was clearly someone considerably older than she was. She at first talked about how mysterious he was, how handsome, but then, the entries took a darker turn. She mentioned hiding when she saw his car arriving, "running as fast as she could" to hide behind the big boxwoods at the side of the house.

One entry mentioned that she had a horrible dream where the man came into her room and watched her sleep, and then two days later, she said that she wasn't sure it was a dream after all.

But it was the next entry that made my blood freeze in my veins:

He was in my room again. This time, he didn't care that I was sleeping. He came over and sat down. He was looking at me all gross, and he put his hand on my blanket, like he was going to pull it down. But just then, I heard Mama walking up the hallway, and I shouted to ask for a glass of water. He looked at me and shook his head. Then he got up and went out the door before Mama came back. When she brought me water, I wanted to tell her he had been here, but she and Daddy are always laughing with him. What if she didn't believe me?

I PUT my finger into the pages of the diary to hold my place and then let my head fall back against the wood behind me. This little girl was about to be assaulted, and even decades later, I could feel the urgency of helping her, saving her.

The next entry scared me for Lily even more:

I don't have a choice. I'm leaving. Mama and Daddy believed me but just told me to tell them the next time it happened. The next time, he's going to trap me, keep me in my room. I know it. I have to run.

The rest of the entry detailed what she was packing and where she was going. Apparently, she had a cousin in Charlottesville, and she thought she could stay there for a little while.

I swallowed hard as I tried to imagine what a young girl would do long-term without help in a new place. I could only hope her cousin's family let her stay, or that her parents took action about this man who was assaulting their daughter. But since that was the last entry in the diary, and I'd found the diary in her house, I didn't think this story had worked out well.

Still, it was more than fifty years ago, and while I knew that the effects of this kind of abuse would be life-long, I decided to hope that Lily had lived a wonderful life, despite this terrible thing so early in her years. I packed the trunk back up and slid it toward the opening in the floor so that I could look through the rest of the items at home, where it wasn't hot enough to boil my skin off.

When I found Mariah in the dining room with a pitcher of iced tea a few minutes later, she was watching Sawyer and Wyatt run through a sprinkler with just their underwear on. The boys were shrieking with delight, and given how hot I was, I couldn't blame them. That looked amazing.

"He's having so much fun," I said as Mariah turned and smiled at me.

"They both are." She pointed to the chair next to me. "Sit. Have some tea. You're as red as a fireball."

I smiled and sat down. "Attics and summer aren't the best combination, but I think I'm done up there." I took a long pull from the iced tea glass. It was perfectly sweet with a hint of mint, just the way I liked it.

"Maybe you could just keep an eye out as the rest of the things come down, flag anything you might think I should see?" I asked. I was fairly confident I'd gotten everything of importance for the sake of history, but there was always the chance I'd missed something.

"Of course," Mariah said. "And our handyman is here today, so why don't I ask him and his assistant to get the things you noted down for us?"

I sighed. "That would be amazing. I wasn't looking forward to that process."

"Consider it done. Your car open?" she asked as she stood and headed toward the kitchen.

"It is. And the back is clear. Please thank them for me," I said as I put the glass of ice against my forehead.

"I will," she said as she turned and walked out the door.

I poured myself another glass of tea and decided to take a look around the dining room since it was one space the Owens had mentioned wanting me to survey but that hadn't been available yet. Outside, I could hear Sawyer and Wyatt still laughing, giving me the best background noise for my work that I could imagine. There was nothing in the world quite like the joy of hearing your child having fun.

The mantel over the original fireplace was made of marble, and while it was simple in design, I knew it was worth a small fortune given its age and the quality of the stone, which looked to be Italian. I ran my fingers over the cool, smooth surface and thought about the expense the Sumners must have gone to do bring this piece of decor across the Atlantic. In an otherwise fairly modest home, this piece was clearly a status symbol, and a beautiful one at that.

Across the top of the mantel, various knick-knacks and other small items were laid out – a clay vase, a beautiful blown glass hummingbird, and an embroidery sampler dated 1823 by Rebecca Sumner. I studied the slightly-askew stitches and smiled. This piece was probably Rebecca's first work, and it was beautiful. I set it on the table to ask Mariah if I could have it.

But it was a small box, inlaid with brass in the shape of a fox that most intrigued me. It looked older, maybe late nineteenth century, but I'd have to study it more to know for sure. At first glance, I thought it was a matchbox since it was about the size of today's business card holders. When I lifted the lid, though, I saw a felt lined box with three tiny compartments. Clearly, not a matchbox then, but I had no idea what it could be. I was going to have to do some research to see what I could find and set the box next to the sampler on the table.

With a quick peek to see that Wyatt and Sawyer had moved on from the sprinkler to digging a massive hole in the backyard and confirmation that Belinda was, indeed, nearby and thus must be in approval – sometimes, digging a whole was a great time-user. My yard was testimony to that – I moved over to what I had been studying from afar every time I'd been in this room – an entire wall of framed photographs.

I knew I would be taking the entire lot of these with me for further research since Mariah and Mark had assured me that they were not of importance to them. But before I packed them up, I took some photos of the layout on the wall, just in case it was of some significance. Then, one by one, I studied each image and laid it on the table, hopeful that Mariah didn't have a need of the table for the next little bit.

Most of the photos were of various people in posed positions – a couple of wedding portraits, some group photos that were clearly posed by a photographer, probably Sumner or his partner, and a few candids from what appeared to be garden parties or picnics. The candids were what caught my attention, as was usually the case for me. Posed images told me how people wanted to be seen, but candids told me about the people in the images themselves.

In one image, two women in broad-brimmed hats were playing what looked like badminton. Both of the women had the porcelain complexion that white women of that time, likely the early twentieth century, treasured so much, and they both grinned with the kind of delight that only comes when adults remember how to play. My favorite part of the image, though, was that the birdie was flying past the head of one of the women. These people were my kindred in athletics, clearly.

Another photo showed four men, all with cigars, lounging

under a tall tree with the edge of a building behind them. I slipped the photo off the wall and walked outside to the front of the house. Sure enough, the tree was one of the tall white oaks that still stood, albeit considerably larger.

The party had been here, then, a fact which sent a ripple of what I thought of as historical energy through me. I was occupying the same space as these people, and since we know that time is an illusion of sorts, I felt like I was, in some way, there with them. The tingle of recognition traveled up and down my spine and left me with goose bumps.

I'd been doing this work long enough now to know that when I had that strong a reaction to a place, my intuition was telling me something that my mind hadn't yet understood. So I took off my shoes by the tree, wiggled my toes into the ground, and took a deep breath. To anyone else, I might have looked a little off, a middle-aged woman barefoot with her arms spread wide as she walked with her eyes closed around the front lawn of a plantation house. But I didn't care, especially since no one was around. This place was telling me something, and I was going to figure out what it was.

I set the photo of the men under the tree where they sat and smiled. If energy traveled through the illusion of time, maybe the men would sense this moment ahead of them. Then, I stepped back and studied the scene again. My beat-up Chucks, the old photograph, the huge tree. Then, something behind the tree caught my eye, probably because I had been lining up my angle of view so that it matched that of the photographer.

There, behind the tree, almost hidden now by the oak's trunk, was a boxwood hedge. Nothing remarkable in that. Most of the old houses around Virginia were littered with boxwoods, alleys, and hedgerows. But it was the narrow arch of light that I could see through the hedge that caught my attention. It looked too tidy to be natural.

I jogged back over to the photograph and looked at it carefully. Sure enough, in the background, the same arch was there, but wider. I quickly slipped my shoes back on since I was long past the days of having my "summer feet" that allowed me to walk on any surface without pain. Then, I slipped sideways through the break in the boxwoods.

A sigh escaped my lips as I stepped into what would only be described as a secret room. The space was small, maybe eight feet by eight feet, but it was completely secluded. In one corner sat a small, metal bench, corroded with rust but still intact. The ground was covered in moss because the entire space was shaded by the oak and the shadow of the house, and if I had to guess, no one had been here in a long time. The boxwoods inside here were ragged, not carefully pruned like the rest of the shrubs, and since the bench was in such poor shape, I imagined it had gone neglected for a few decades. I couldn't wait to show Sawyer and Wyatt and then Mariah and Mark.

But given that my skin was still tingling, I didn't go to find anyone yet. I couldn't shake the sensation that this place had something it wanted me to see. I walked over and tested the bench, and when it seemed to be sturdy, I lowered myself onto it and took a deep breath as I scanned the shrub walls around me.

It was only on my third scan of the bushes that I noticed it, a little concave space in the corner opposite where I sat, just to the left of where I'd come into the room. I walked over and knelt down, and there, I saw them covered by the decades of growth, two small stones, half-buried in the earth.

I lay down on the ground to look more closely, and I could just make out the faintest white markings on the stone. I pushed my head into the stiff branches and dug out my phone. When the flash went off, I knew I was right. There were words on these stones.

And when I looked at the pictures, I swallowed a scream.

There, on one stone were the words Baby Sumner, 1856. And on the other, Lily, 1980.

These were graves.

I RUSHED INSIDE and found Mariah, where she was guiding the workmen down the final flight of stairs with the trunk I'd found with Lily's things in it. I asked them to stop and put the trunk down in the dining room. "You need to see something," I said.

Mariah studied me a minute before directing the men to finish bringing the items down, and then she followed me out the side door and up around the house. I quickly showed her the room and then the two stones. "Look," I said as I held up the photograph I'd taken.

"Oh my word," she said as her hand flew to her mouth. "Are these...."She didn't finish.

"I think so," I shook my head. "Although, it's odd, given how close they are to the house." I didn't know quite what to make of this all, but I knew we needed to figure it out. "I have something else to show you," I said and led her back into the dining room.

There, I quickly took out Lily's diary and, because now they seemed especially important, the clothes I'd found with it. The rest of the trunk was full, too, and I knew Mariah and I were going to go through it imminently. But first, I needed to catch her up.

We sat down on the floor, and I handed her the diary. She didn't ask me a thing, just opened it up and began to read. Meanwhile, I started lifting out each item in the trunk, studying the various blankets and sets of curtains carefully before laying them aside. It didn't appear there was anything else of importance in here, but I was definitely going to triple check.

When Mariah finished reading, she set the diary on the floor behind her and said, "Someone killed her."

I stared at her a moment. "Is that what you think?"

She shook her head quickly. "I don't know what to think, but given her last entry and the grave...."

I sighed. "Yeah." I didn't know what else to say.

"Can I see that photo again, the one you took?" Her voice was quiet but steady.

I handed her my phone after opening it to the image again. "We need a better look at those stones."

She nodded as she looked carefully at the screen. "Do you think that says 1856?" She held up the screen and pointed to the stone that said "Baby Sumner."

"That's what I see," I said as I leaned closer to be sure. "Why?"

Mariah handed me the phone and then stood up. At the side table, she picked up the stack of memorial photos and walked back over before folding herself to the floor beside me. She slipped through the photos quickly and then stopped at one of a tiny baby in a long christening gown. If I hadn't known better, I would have thought the child was sleeping.

"Look on the back," Mariah said as she handed me the photo card.

The handwritten script on the back read, "Clayton Sumner, 1856." I sighed. "Oh, how sad."

Mariah nodded. "It is. We need to figure out where he falls in the Sumner family tree."

"That shouldn't be hard, and I'd like to find that out about Lily, too." Something wasn't feeling right, beyond the sad horror of what we'd just discovered. I couldn't shake the fact that people just didn't bury people close to their homes, for lots of reasons, not the least of which was sanitation. "It just seems so odd to bury two people that close to the house," I finally said when I gathered my thoughts enough to speak.

"That wasn't typical?" Mariah asked.

"No, maybe for an infant, I could see it. The parents wanting to keep the baby close, even in death. But for a girl...."

Mariah sighed. "So what do we do?"

I had just begun asking myself that question. "Well, first I need to call Santiago. He needs to see this just in case." I tapped the diary. "Then, I expect we need to do some research."

"What about clearing back the boxwoods a bit, getting a better look at the, um, graves?" Mariah's face was flushed.

I nodded. "I expect that's a good idea, but let's see what Santi says first, okay?" I really didn't want to call him again, not for another possible murder, even if this one was not quite as old as the possible murder of Mr. Julius Sumner by his wife.

Santi's voice went from gentle to tired as soon as I told him what I'd found. I knew the revelation of all these historical secrets was wearing on him. He had enough to do as sheriff with current crime, much less these long-ago mysteries that, without me, would have been left long-buried. Quite literally.

"You okay?" He asked after I gave him all the details. "This is a lot."

I smiled into the phone. Even with all the work this meant for him, he still thought about me. I'd never had that before in my life, and his thoughtfulness gave me a kind of stability and security I hadn't really known was possible. "I am. But yes, this is a lot. See you soon?"

"Already on my way out the door," he said.

While we waited for Santiago to arrive, Mariah and I put the blankets and curtains back into the trunk and then carried it to the car. Rob and his assistant had already moved the other few boxes into the back of the Subaru, and so we slid the trunk in beside those and then went to sit down on the front porch.

I was antsy with all that could be done – genealogical research, cutting back boxwoods to see what was around those stones, more reading of journals and diaries to see what we could put together about what I could only imagine was two murders... at least. I wasn't willing to let myself think that baby Clayton had been killed, but I knew that sometimes post-partum depression took no prisoners.

Still, I also knew that Santi needed to look around before we did anything. He'd be here any minute, and until then, we'd just have to wait.

Fortunately, the best distraction in the world came tearing around the far side of the house in his underwear just after we sat down. Sawyer was wielding a slingshot, and inside it was a water balloon... and from the look of glee on his face, I knew I was the target. I'd never been so happy to be smacked with cold water in my life.

5

———————

Santi's perusal of the small graveyard, as I was now thinking of it despite my best efforts to keep an open mind, was brief. "We'll need to trim back these shrubs, get a better look."

Mariah and Mark, who had come right home from work when his wife called, nodded somberly and then asked a very smart question. "How do you want us to handle that? Do it ourselves? Have a professional come in?"

Despite his obvious stress, Santi smiled just a bit. "Let's have a professional do it. That way we don't risk disturbing the site, *and* you get a fresh trim instead of a butcher job." He winced. "Not that you two would butcher—"

Mark interrupted. "Oh, we would. No offense taken. Professional landscapers we are not." He took out his phone and quickly found the number. "Linda, is your team available today for an emergency? Of course, we'll pay your rush rate."

I took a moment and imagined what kind of situations required landscapers to have a rush rate. I could see real needs – trees across roads or on roofs, a sudden discovery of a poison ivy patch before a child's birthday party, apparently the discovery of graves under bushes. But I couldn't help but think their usual rush calls involved uneven patches of grass, rogue dandelions, and perhaps the refusal of zinnias to bloom in the right color palette. The idea of the burly, strong folks I knew who were landscapers standing in front of a flower bed and having to explain that they could not change the hot pink to bright orange at will gave me a little inward laugh, a much needed relief.

When Mark hung up, he said, "They'll be here in fifteen. Linda and her crew are the best, and they are discreet."

Again, I had to wonder for just a moment about what sort of situations required discretion from a landscaper and quickly decided I probably didn't want to know. "What do we do in the meantime?"

"Let's eat," Mariah said. "I have a ham in the kitchen, and we can make some sandwiches." She turned to me. "Sawyer will eat ham?"

"Just put some slices on a plate, and he's good to go." It was one of the few foods, along with bacon, that I could count on for my son to devour. "Do you have any grapes, by chance?" I didn't want him to be pure carnivore.

"Always. Let's ask Belinda to get them dried off and redressed, and we'll set out lunch," Mariah casually looped her arm through mine and led me to the back door while the men stayed in the garden square to strategize.

It's possible that Sawyer and Wyatt actually sat down for a partial second to eat, but they moved so quickly in an effort to get on to the game of hide and seek that Belinda had promised them that I mostly saw a whiz of color and ham flying off plates. For her part, Belinda looked quite content to carry the sandwich that Mariah had made out the door after the boys. She was clearly a child's caretaker at heart.

The men joined us, and we all ate our sandwiches in silence until we heard the sound of a truck pulling up outside. Our food was left abandoned, and largely untouched, while we hurried outside to meet Linda and her crew.

While Mark went to ask the handyman Rob to bring around some tarps for the crew to use to pull away the debris from their work, Mariah guided the landscapers to the pocket of boxwoods, where they all stood and listened as Mariah and Santi described what needed to be done.

Linda was a red-headed woman with skin so pale she looked like she burned when the sun came up, but given the strong scent of sunscreen and her broad-brimmed hat, it seemed she also knew how to take care of herself. She had the build of a dancer, all sinewy muscle and grace, but I expected she could outlift some of the strong men I had in my life. "All right, guys, let's move quickly but carefully. No standing on the possible graves if we can help it, okay?"

The men, all around our age with the muscles and tans of people who work hard outside all day, moved quickly toward the tools they'd set outside the boxwood wall. Two brought in huge loppers, and the third had a set of hand pruners. Linda took one pair of loppers and made four cuts on the shrub just above the stones, immediately opening up the space to light.

As the team made quick work of clearing out above and around the stones, Rob brought two bright blue tarps into the small space, a space clearly not designed to hold the eight people now inside it. I stepped out and Santi followed, so that the team had more space to work.

The two of us made our way to a shady patch of lawn and sat down where we could be found easily, but also have a bit of privacy. "This is all so... so..." -- I couldn't quite find the words -- "...so much."

Santi nodded. "It is. We have a possible murder from 150 years ago. We have a possible death of a young girl fifty years ago. We have a possible infant's burial." He looked at me. "Am I missing anything?"

I sighed. "Just those creepy photos of the dead people, but I'm not sure those are related."

"Oh, right. Well, let's not rule anything out at this point. All this seems to be far too much weird even for a Southern family." He shook his head.

I smiled. I didn't know an old house in Virginia that didn't come with its fair share of stories about extreme psychological states or gruesome death. If you didn't have a ghost story to go with your antebellum architecture then you weren't truly Southern, I figured. But this house, this family, it had taken all the Southern Gothic traditions and wrapped them up into one place. If I'd seen the ghost of a woman in a ball gown at the window above us, I wouldn't have been surprised.

Fortunately, the ghosts stayed hidden, at least the spiritual ones did. But just as I was about to lean back and close my eyes for a moment while we waited, Rob and Linda came around the corner of the boxwoods and stood on the opposite side of the oak from us. Given their hushed voices, I figured they didn't see us, and when Santi put a finger to his lips, I didn't protest. Eavesdropping wasn't really eavesdropping when the people came to you.

"What are you doing?" Rob said in a rancor-filled whisper. "We all promised our parents we'd leave this be."

I sat up and Santiago put his hand on my arm to keep me from making any more sudden movements.

"We did, Rob. But what am I supposed to say when they call my company for help? 'No, I'm sorry. I can't do that bit of hedge trimming for you because I promised my mommy." Linda's voice was firm but quiet.

Rob let out a long sigh. "I know. I'm in the same boat, but this is part of why we've stayed on here at this place, right? Part of why we've worked so hard to get to the new owners."

I looked over at Santiago, and his pensive expression held me in my place. If he wasn't moving to ask what they were talking about, there had to be a good reason.

"I know. I know," Linda's voice suddenly sounded weary. "But they've found them now. Isn't it better that I stay close? Keep an eye on things?"

Rob was pacing now, moving back and forth just ten feet from where Santiago and I sat stock-still. "Yeah, I guess. But we have to let everyone else know. We might have to do something if this gets out of hand," Rob whispered.

"Yeah. Let everyone know, okay? We'll get together ASAP and figure out what's next." She took off her hat and wiped sweaty red strands from her forehead. "I don't know why we're still keeping this so secret. It was such a long time ago."

"Hatred has a long shelf life," Rob said as he walked back toward the front of the house.

Linda stood fanning herself with her hat for a few moments and then turned back toward the garden hedge.

As soon as she was out of sight, I stood up and began to pace myself. "What was that all about?" I said to myself as much as to Santi.

He stood and put his hands on the back of his head. "I have no idea, but until we figure out more about this situation, it seems best to leave them to their secrets. If we begin to ask questions too soon, then we risk locking everyone down even tighter."

I sighed. "Right. Are we telling Mark and Mariah?"

Santi shook his head. "No. Let's keep this between us. No need to make them play a role with their staff." He turned toward me. "Are you up for research?"

I smiled and rolled my eyes. "When am I not up for research?"

"I know you know this, but we have to keep this work quiet. You, Ms. Nicholas, and Mika, that's it," he said quietly.

"And me," I hope, Savannah Wilson said from behind me. "Right?" Santiago's deputy looked at him and then at me and widened her eyes. "Right?!"

"Of course," Santi said. "I'll catch you up back at the station. You okay to keep an eye on things here?" he asked me.

I nodded, even as the increasing weight of what was to be a dream job settled more firmly on my shoulders. "I'll see you for dinner." I turned to Savannah. "It's sloppy joe night. Want to join us?"

She glanced over at Santi, who gave a small nod. "Sure. Give us a chance to talk."

At that exact moment, Sawyer ran between us with Wyatt close on his tail with what looked to be a small snake in his tiny hands. "No, no, no," Sawyer squealed in delight.

"At least they're having fun," I said.

Santi squeezed my shoulders and winked at me. "Now, come on. You know you love a good mystery as much as anyone. Do your thing, woman." He kissed my cheek, and I couldn't help but smile. He was right. As heavy as this situation was, I was going to enjoy the process of digging in.

FORTUNATELY, the rest of the afternoon went quietly, well, except for the four-year-olds running around the house like they were being chased by demons. To their credit, they were chasing each other with various and sundry living creatures – beetles, roly-polys, earthworms – but somehow, I didn't think they were as much terrified as they were delighted by faux terror.

Linda's team diligently cleared out around the stones and then seamlessly trimmed the rest of the hedge square to match. When they were done, the space was four feet longer and wider than it had been, but it somehow looked identical to when I'd found it. They were definitely good at their work.

I didn't see Rob for the rest of the afternoon, and while that probably meant he was simply doing the work assigned to him by the Owens, I couldn't help but think it might be because he was having a clandestine meeting with whoever he and Linda were colluding with.

UNFORTUNATELY, Santi didn't lay my suspicions to rest at dinner. Apparently, he'd looked for Rob under the ruse of just needing some time in the fresh air and asking Mark if he minded if he poked around the property. "I'm not sure Mark bought it, but he didn't ask any questions. Still, the bottom line is that I think I went pretty much everywhere on that estate, and I didn't see any sign of him. I think it's pretty likely he had stepped away to meet with whoever he and Linda were talking about."

Sawyer, who had just polished off an entire box of macaroni and cheese by himself while watching videos of kids not much older than he was doing ninja warrior training courses, hadn't missed a beat. "Do you think Rob is a bandit?" he asked.

Bandits equaled "bad guys" in Saw's book, and clearly he was more astute at picking up undertones of conversations than I had previously given him credit for. "No, Love Bug. Rob is the person who works for Wyatt's parents. Santi just wanted to talk to him but couldn't find him today."

"Because he was hiding?" Saw asked with wide eyes and all the imagination a young child can muster.

Santi said, "Maybe. Where do you think he might have been hiding?"

"Under a big, big, big rock," Sawyer said, returning us to the world of the preschooler, where anything is possible and most things unlikely.

"Could've been," Santi said. "Do you want to find me?"

Sawyer jumped up. "I'll count."

While the boys sprinted around the house and the yard, one not quite hiding before the other came to find him, I cleaned up the kitchen and then settled myself back at the table with a mug of tea and my laptop. I began by sending Mika and Ms. Nicholas a comprehensive email, with photos, about what we'd found at the Sumner Place today and asking if they would please think about what they might know. I also cautioned them, per Santi's instructions, to keep this quiet.

Then, thankful for my subscription, I opened up my newspaper database and did a search for the dates from the tombstones and then for the names on those stones. I didn't turn up anything, not even a mention of a death or a missing child in any of the local papers or the larger regional ones either. I'd kind of expected that for the infant. Sadly, infant death was far too common to warrant news coverage, even now.

But that there was nothing on Lily's death, or at least her disappearance, bothered me. Surely, the disappearance of a teenage daughter from a wealthy family would get coverage, even fifty years ago when news wasn't quite as pervasive as it is now. But there was no mention of the Sumners beyond listings as donors or mentions in church activity articles. Nothing at all about Lily.

That, even more than the gravestones hidden in a secret garden hedge, made me suspicious. Something was going on here, and I was going to figure it out.

Clearly, Ms. Nicholas and Mika agreed because within minutes, they had both replied with a commitment to think on the possibilities. "I'll get into the archives first thing tomorrow," Ms. Nicholas also said. "I'd go tonight, but I don't want to raise suspicions...." She let her message trail off there.

She was right. In a place as small and gossip-driven as Octonia, the historical society director showing up after hours to do research would draw attention. Most people wouldn't gossip out of any kind of maliciousness, but things that were out of the ordinary here were big news, mostly because there wasn't much other news.

And if people got wind that we had found two gravestones in the boxwoods at the Sumner Place, they would have reason to talk. In this case, talking could be particularly bad since it would alert Rob, Linda, and whoever their associates were to the fact that we were investigating. Surely they knew we would. Santi hadn't exactly hidden his presence there today, but no one needed to know we were going back into the records to find information. That level of commitment would indicate that this was a full-on investigation, a murder investigation.

Sawyer asked if Santi could put him to bed that night, and I gladly obliged, eager to dig a little further into what documents I could find online to look for hints and the stories here. Since the newspapers had been a bust, I decided to look at the census to see what details I could figure out about the baby and about Lily Sumner.

The baby turned out to be a baby boy named Simon, who had died after just eight days. The cause of death was listed as Asphyxia, and while it was likely the child had died from SIDS, long before SIDS was known to be a concern for infants, I couldn't help but think about his mother's mental illness and the possible threat she posed to her own child. If she had killed her husband, maybe it wasn't outside the range of possibility that she could kill her baby.

I shook my head and shivered after that thought coalesced. I wasn't wrong, but I knew it was far harder to even dislike your child than it was to loathe someone you had once loved romantically. I had never considered killing Sawyer's father, but I had felt some pretty awful things toward him before I'd made the sensible decision for all of us and ended the marriage. Never once, though, even when he was pushing on my last viable strand of patience, had I felt an urge to harm Sawyer. Even in the throes of postpartum depression, my mothering instinct had trumped the deep sadness and exhaustion. Sadly, I knew that wasn't the case for all women, and maybe it wasn't the case for Mrs. Sumner.

Still, it didn't seem likely I was going to find clarity on that fact through public records, so I turned my research to Lily. As a child born in the years just before the tech boom, more might be known about her, not as much as would eventually be available for people to know about someone Sawyer's age, of course, but more than about an eight-day-old infant who lived in the nineteenth century for sure.

Very quickly, I found a birth certificate for Lily Sumner. She had been born on June 9, and had been 9 lbs 5 ounces, a big baby girl. I found a couple further mentions of her in newspaper articles, once when she'd dressed as a pilgrim in kindergarten and then again in third grade when she'd won the spelling bee. From all I could see, she had been a healthy, successful, happy child.

But then, the record stopped. No further newspaper mentions, no further public records like I would have expected. No marriage certificate or military enlistment forms. No listing of her name on birth certificates for her children. And, most significantly to my mind, no death certificate. That absence felt striking because surely her parents had reported her death, as was required by law.

I did a few alternate searches using various spellings and orderings of her name, but nothing at all came up. In terms of public records, it looked like Lily Sumner had simply disappeared at age 11, which seemed to align with the gravestone outside the house but not with the facts of a child's death. Something was amiss, but I couldn't yet put my finger on what.

. . .

WHEN SANTIAGO CAME DOWN a few minutes after I hit my dead end, I poured us each a cup of chamomile tea and pointed to the front porch. "Care to rock?" I said with a wink.

"I like your definition of *rock*," he said as he held up the front door for me. "It's nice and slow."

I settled down into my rocking chair and laughed. "I don't really have a high speed setting anymore."

"Me neither," he said as he sat next to me. "Find anything?"

I told him the scant details my research had turned up and shook my head. "I get that the death of an infant back in that time would have been considered sad but tragically normal, but the death of a pre-teen girl in the early 80's? Surely that would have made the news, especially in a family as prominent as the Sumners."

Santiago nodded. "You'd think. And you know, we'd probably remember it, too. She died, if the tombstone is accurate, in 1980, right? I would have been 8, so you were 6."

I nodded. "I don't remember hearing anything about this at all, do you?" In our small community, even children heard the worst news. It became gossip at school and coffee time conversation at church. When I was four, a pastor's daughter at a nearby church had gotten pregnant before she was married, and when I'd heard, I asked my mom why everybody was so upset since that meant she got to have a baby to play with. My mom was mortified.

"Nope, not a word," Santiago said. "Let's check with Mika."

I texted her immediately to ask if she had heard anything about a little girl dying when we were kids. Her response was immediate: *Not a word.*

I showed Santi my phone and then shook my head. "Something is definitely going on here, but I don't think it's that a little girl died and no one knew."

He nodded. "I agree. We need to talk to Rob and Linda. You free tomorrow to interview them?"

"Sure. What do you think about giving Ms. Nicholas a heads up and inviting her, too?" I knew my friend would do extensive research in the archives to find what she could about Lily Sumner's, what I was now calling in my mind, "disappearance."

"Good idea. Let's set our meeting at 2, and I'll ask Mariah and Mark to arrange things with Linda and Rob so that it seems more generally about the graves than about our specific questions." He picked up his phone and pushed the screen.

Somehow I didn't think we were really getting ahead of anything here with our caginess, but given the speed of gossip around this community, it was definitely better to keep facts close to our vest until we need to flash them.

SAWYER WENT off to school with a literal skip in his step because it was field trip day. He and his schoolmates were going to see a theater demonstration in the county park, and while I was thrilled for the arts exposure, Sawyer was mostly excited that he got to ride in the school van with only a seatbelt and not a car seat. Talk about adventure.

I spent the morning organizing my notes about baby Simon and Lily, and then I put together a timeline of the Sumner family so that we could keep who was who and when straight. All my prep work for our meeting done, I drove myself to my shop, where Claire was doing her top-notch sales work on a gentleman who looked like he had just stepped out of a 1920s tobacconists' shop. He had on a fedora with a white feather in the red band, clenched a pipe (thankfully unlit) in his teeth, and had on suspenders that looked far more about fashion than function.

Claire was in full spiel as she described the history of a gorgeous brushed-brass chandelier I had picked up from a salvage job over in Dayton a few weeks back. She recounted the original home's history as a railroad baron's house, talked about the craftsmanship of the piece, and suggested it would make a great addition to his Arts and Crafts style bungalow.

I did my best to be inconspicuous as I headed past them in the hallway and quietly ducked into my office, but Claire caught my eye just as I was about to shut my office door. "Paisley, do you have a minute?" she said.

I stifled a groan and pulled up my best fake smile before saying, "Sure, of course." I stepped back through the door and put out my hand. "I'm Paisley Sutton. Thanks for shopping at our store."

The man extended his dark brown hand and said, "My pleasure. Ms. Sutton. Wesley Bourne. Your staff is well-informed about your merchandise." He turned back to Claire. "Please pack the chandelier up for me. I'd like to take it when I go."

Claire beamed as he handed her a credit card.

"Thank you, Mr. Bourne," I said. "That's a lovely piece."

"Yes, it is, and it'll be a fine addition to my house, but I really came to see you, Ms. Sutton. May I have a minute?" He pointed behind me toward my office door.

I looked over his shoulder to Claire, who was now frowning as she slipped the chandelier off the hook from which it hung. "Claire, let us know when Mr. Bourne's purchase is ready?"

"Yes, ma'am," she said with a stiff nod as she held my gaze. She understood that I didn't want to be with our guest long, and I was grateful for the power of silent communication.

"Please, come this way, Mr. Bourne," I said as I turned back into my office. As I made my way around my desk, he sat down in one of the wooden dining chairs I had set in front of it. Mostly those chairs were used for me to set things on, but they did hold people, at least I hoped they did.

When the wooden frame didn't collapse under Mr. Bourne's

weight, I let out a small sigh of relief and sat down myself. "What can I do for you, sir?"

He looked around the room a moment and then met my eyes again. "Can I trust that what I share with you will be kept in the strictest of confidence?"

In movies, this is where the person being asked always swears they will keep the secret, but given my experience with secrets and my engagement to the local sheriff, I had a whole lot of hesitations about making such promises. "Mr. Bourne, I can assure you that I am discreet and do not share anything with anyone who does not need to know the information. But if what you want is a confidentiality promise from me, I cannot give you that, I'm afraid."

One corner of his mouth turned up. "Good," he said. "Forgive my little test, but I needed to know you weren't already, well should we say, touched by what I'm about to share."

I leaned forward and put my elbows on the table. "Well, now you certainly have my attention," I said. "What *do* you have to share?"

He mimicked my body position and quietly said, "I understand you've found our Lily's 'grave.'" He made air quotes as he said the word *grave*.

I leaned further toward him and said, "Yes, we did. Can I ask how you know that?"

"You can, and I will tell you. But first, I need to clarify something for you. Lily Sumner is not dead."

I sat back so hard that my desk chair rolled a few feet back. After I had scooted myself back to the desk, I said, "She's not?" I tried to sound incredulous, but given the lack of evidence I'd found in the records through my research, I wasn't really that surprised. Mr. Bourne didn't need to know that though.

"No, she's not." He tilted his head and looked at me. "I think you probably already ascertained as much, if you're as astute as folks tell me you are." He winked at me and then continued. "She is alive and well and living just over the mountain in Harrisonburg under a new name and with a rich and full life."

I nodded as I tried to absorb all this information as well as figure out why he was telling me this. "Okay, well, that's good to know, but why is there a tombstone with her name on it at the Sumner Place, then?"

"That, my dear, is precisely why I am here." He laid his warm hand over mine on the desk. "Before I tell you more, I do need one assurance if you can make it."

"If I can give it, I will," I said as I nodded.

"If at all possible, please leave Mrs. Sumner in peace. She wishes no ill will to Octonia, but she does wish to stay separate from her homeplace in every way." He held my gaze as I thought about what he said.

The young woman's journal came to mind, and I couldn't help but wonder if the fear she'd expressed there was why she wanted to stay away now. "Is she in hiding?" I didn't want to reveal stories that were not mine to tell, but I also wanted to understand the gravity of Mr. Bourne's request because it seemed quite grave.

"She was," he replied. "For many years, and given that you ask that question, I suspect you may know why."

I sighed. "I found her childhood journal. She described some, well, horrific experiences there. I do hope she found respite from them."

Mr. Bourne smiled. "She did, and while she no longer needs to be as secretive as she once did, she still does not, as you can imagine, wish to delve into that part of her past." He squeezed my fingers. "I'm sure you can understand."

"Completely," I said. "I am happy to return her journal to her if she'd like."

"I will ask," Bourne replied, "but she has never mentioned it or any concern about anyone finding it." He took a deep breath.

"It's not as if people didn't know, after all." He sounded so weary that I put my other hand over his.

"No one believed her?" I asked, not wanting to pry but unable to stop myself from wanting to understand this woman's pain.

Bourne shook his head. "That's not quite it. People believed her. Her parents believed her, but they also didn't." He pulled his hand away and sat back.

I studied his face. "I'm sorry. I don't understand."

He looked up at the ceiling for a minute. "I guess it's a matter of the degree of belief they had. No one doubted that something had happened between Lily and Do—," he interrupted himself and glanced at me, "and her abuser. But the characterization of what happened differed. Lily was abused by this adult man. But her parents chose to see the encounters as mutual, a relationship of sorts."

My stomach plummeted. "But if he was an adult, that's—"

Bourne put up a hand. "Statutory rape. Yes. But someone had to press charges, and Lily was II." He tugged at his suspenders briefly. "Lily is not interested in seeking justice for herself. She has done what she has needed to do for herself, but she is interested – had always been dedicated to having her story be a cautionary tale that protects other young women."

This desire felt both noble and profoundly sad to me. I understood it though. If Lily could not gain justice against her abuser, then at least she could help women in similar situations. I understood that completely. "How can I help?"

Bourne smiled. "She would like you to uncover and share as much of her early life story as possible." At this, he placed an expanding folder on the desk. "You already have her journal, and she has written down as much information as she can about her story without naming names."

I stared at the folder on my desk. "She doesn't want me to identify her abuser?"

"No." He looked me straight in the eye. "She does not."

Goosebumps ran up the back of my arms. "She's protecting him?"

"She's protecting herself," he said matter-of-factly. "This is her one requirement, Ms. Sutton. I do hope you can honor it."

I sat back in my chair and took a deep breath. I didn't know the statute of limitations on sexual assault of a minor, but I imagined it was long past. And I also believed that women should be able to make their own choices, especially about their bodies, even if I disagreed with their choices. "Okay, I can do that," I said. "But I want to be clear that if by chance, in the course of my research, I find out about other victims, I will need to speak with her - or with you as her proxy – to determine if we need to bring in law enforcement."

"Agreed," Bourne said, "And I spoke with Sheriff Shifflett about this situation this morning. He is aware of Lily's wishes and has agreed unless there is cause to bring charges pursuant to an actionable case."

I let out a long sigh. If Santiago had agreed, then I felt even more confident in my decision to do the same. "I'm glad to hear that." I pulled the folder to my side of the desk. "I'll look through the material she sent and... "I realized I had no idea what to do if I had questions.

Bourne reached into his breast pocket and pulled out a business card. "You can reach me via email or phone if you have any questions for Lily. We do ask, though, that you limit your questions to facts that you cannot ascertain on your own. She does not want to offer opinions or personal anecdotes of any sort."

I took his card and gave a single nod. "Understood." I stood as he did, and we shook hands again. "I'll be in touch in a few days with an update."

"No need. We will see the article when it comes out, and if you need us before then, you know how to reach me." He put his hat on his head, tipped it toward me, and then walked out of my office where I heard him say, quite brightly, "Now, Claire, let me pay for my chandelier."

The whole conversation was so odd that I didn't even know what to make of it beyond the fact that if this was a way I could help Lily, I would do it to the best of my ability. But I didn't have a lot of time to think about the adult woman behind this request since I wanted to be familiar with the materials she sent before our 2 p.m. meeting at the Sumner Place with Linda and Rob. I had two hours before the meeting. If I skipped lunch, I might just have enough time to read the stack of papers I pulled out of the folder. Maybe.

6

———

An hour and what felt like a thousand stomach growls later, Santiago walked into my office with two to-go containers and two Styrofoam cups. The scent of fried food wafted in with him, and I almost groaned in delight. "Burgers?" I said as I took one container from him.

"Of course. I figured that since you'd talked to Bourne, you might be buried in paper and not have time to eat." Santi and I had texted since Bourne left because I'd wanted to be sure all was on the up-and-up with the situation, at least as best we could tell. My fiancé seemed to think so, and he was a far warier participant in most things than I was. So if he felt this was legit, I was in. As he set a pile of napkins next to me, he looked at the piles of paper I'd made and said, "Wow. That's a lot of information."

"So much information," I said. From what I had gleaned, as I told Santi, from the material that Lily had sent over, the man who had abused her had groomed her first, as was typical, and then had done the usually despicable act of convincing her that if she told anyone, then they'd think she was a horrible person, an immoral girl more specifically. Most of that information came to Lily, it seemed, later in life after what she described as extensive therapy and work on her trauma, but through that work, she was able to provide very detailed accounts of what had happened to her where. Given that I now knew the Sumner Place pretty well, it hadn't been hard for me to envision the spaces in which this man had assaulted this little girl. It was so hard to simply read about that I couldn't imagine how Lily had survived, much less been able to record her memories so cogently.

"For a bit," I told Santiago with a fair amount of shame, "I thought of all those cases from a few years back that got press because they were supposedly based on 'recovered' memories that were said to have been implanted by therapists. Given how fuzzy my memory is about my childhood, I had trouble believing Lily could remember so accurately."

Santi tilted his head. "What changed your mind about her memories?"

I let out a hard breath. "Honestly, it was two things. One, I've read her journal from that time, and the dates and descriptions line up. Two, I've had experiences of remembering things from my own childhood that I had thought were lost to history, and sometimes I can remember them with so much detail that it feels like I'm in the place again with scents, sounds, and temperature to boot."

My fiancé stood up and walked behind me to begin rubbing my shoulders. "Painful things?" he asked.

I shook my head. "Usually not, but there are just some memories that are so vivid – like the time Benny Willett passed me a 'Do you like me note" on the seventh concrete step of the wide stairway that went from the bus hallway to the cafeteria – that they carry a really big weight."

"Is this Benny guy anyone I need to worry about?" Santi said as he eased a knot out of my left shoulder.

"Nah. I checked the box for No." I put my hand over his.

"But the fact that I remember the moment tells me it matters somehow in a crucial way, and it's not even traumatic." I did have some hard memories, some really painful ones, and Santi knew about many, but not all of those. Some I just wasn't ready to delve into yet, which was why I was so very impressed with Lily's ability to go back into these experiences. Maybe creating a whole new life before this trauma was one way of getting free of it.

Santi sat back down and pulled a stack of paper toward him. "I see what you mean." He read through the top sheet in the stack. "What's this pile?" He tapped the papers.

"That's everything Lily had to say about her parents' response when she told them what was happening. From what she said, she told them about the abuse three different times – once when it first started to scare her, once after he visited her room the first time, and once just before she ran away."

"How long a time period are we talking here?" Santi's brow was deeply furrowed.

"About four months from the start of his attention to when she ran away. Her parents grew increasingly dismissive of her concerns the more intense the abuse got." I shuddered at the thought of Sawyer being harmed this way and felt absolutely nauseated at the idea that I would ignore or downplay his experience if he told me about it. I couldn't even let my mind go long down that path of speculation. It was far too dark.

"So for four months, her parents denied her experience? Is that why she ran away?" Santi asked with a bite to his words.

"Seems it was a big part of it, but the real impetus was that she thought he might kidnap her." One of the things that Lily had sent to me via Bourne was a copy of her journal that began, as indicated by the dates on the pages, right after she ran away.

"What?! Who is this guy?" Santi's voice was outright angry now.

I shook my head. "I don't know, and Bourne was explicit that she didn't want us trying to find out." I had been quite angry myself when I read the accounts, and I was still seething pretty good. But as someone who knew what it was, in a much less serious way than this, to have people I cared about dismiss my experiences of assault, I understood how much heartache it might cause her to have, in any way, to confront her abuser. "Besides, as you told him, the statute of limitations has expired on any crimes that were committed."

A muscle flicked in Santi's jaw. "Yes, but that doesn't mean I don't want to know who this guy is. Chances are he's still alive and probably still living here. He's a predator, and—"

I interrupted him. "I don't disagree, but we gave her our word. Now, we need to focus on telling her story well." I reached over and took his hand. "And maybe, if we're lucky, the truth will out itself without our direct efforts." I was putting a fair amount of hope into this idea myself. "Plus, it seems like Lily took some actions to protect other girls and women. She's pretty vague about what exactly she did, but it sounds like whatever she did might have permanently hampered this jerk's ability to harm anyone else."

Santiago smiled. "I like this woman." He shook his head. "I mean, there are other forms of justice besides the law, I suppose."

I patted his hand. "Yes, and one of them is becoming a very successful woman who overcomes what some man did to her."

"Oh yeah?" Santi said and watched my face eagerly as he waited for me to explain.

"For obvious reasons, she's not very forthright about the details. For example, I don't know what field she works in or the organizations she's helped found and fund, but last year, Lily says her foundations donated over $8,000,000 to organizations that help protect victims of sexual assault."

"Holy cow," Santi said with a whistle. "That's a lot of money to donate, which means she brings in a lot of money each year."

"Definitely, and she's not shy about sharing the fact that she owns several houses in several countries, employs over forty people to take care of her and those houses, and runs at least three successful businesses. This woman is wealthy, and she's proud of her wealth." I felt a shiver of admiration sneak up my back. "She kicks tail."

"Yeah, she does," Santiago said before glancing at his watch. "Let's go share her story with our friends and see what else they've dug up." He held out his hand and helped me to my feet.

I gathered all the papers with binder clips and then slipped them back into Bourne's envelope before tucking it and my laptop into my messenger bag and following Santiago to his cruiser. I was still apprehensive about what Rob and Linda might tell us this afternoon, but knowing that Lily had survived and thrived made any other news a little more bearable.

WHEN WE ARRIVED at the Sumner Place, we found Mariah, Mark, and Ms. Nicholas already set up at a long picnic table under one of the white oaks in front of the house. There was a pitcher of iced tea with long sprigs of mint spinning in it and a pound cake that looked just about perfect. If we weren't here to talk about two gravestones, it would have been a lovely afternoon gathering with friends.

And it felt that way for a few minutes as we all poured each other drinks and cut pieces of the lemon-iced cake and caught up on the small talk of Octonia, but as soon as Rob and Linda walked around the corner of the house, their faces pale and drawn, the mood took a far more somber tone. Clearly, these two were not here for a casual chat.

I had hoped that maybe the mysterious "she" that Santiago and I had overheard them mention before was Lily and that she or Bourne had let them know we were in contact. But since they appeared reticent and withdrawn and refused even a glass of iced tea on a 95 degree day, I decided this wasn't likely.

At many a gathering of Southerners, someone would be asked to pray, but since I had no idea what Mark and Mariah's religious leanings were and since I knew Ms. Nicholas to be staunchly atheist, I decided maybe the best way to start was to talk about why we were here. I asked Mariah and Mark to describe why they'd brought me into their new home. Then, I mentioned that I had overheard Linda and Rob talking about the gravestones the day before, and I was hoping they might share what they knew with us.

I purposefully stayed vague, following the strategy Santi had suggested on the way over. He thought it best we invite them to participate in our inquiry instead of accusing them of hiding something, and he had also suggested he simply be on hand casually but that he would, unless necessary, stay quiet. To that end, he had also changed into jeans and a polo for the afternoon.

Sadly, our strategy didn't have the desired effect of immediately relaxing Linda and Rob, or at least not enough that they began to volunteer information. So I moved on with the loose agenda I had set in my mind. "Ms. Nicholas, were you able to uncover anything about either of these gravestones?" I was eager to hear what she'd found, but I was glad I'd decided not to show my hand about Lily's materials yet. Hopefully, Ms. Nicholas's meticulous work would back up what I had discovered this morning.

"Well, let me begin with Lily Sumner. I can tell you almost nothing about her except that she was raised in this house, that she had what appears to be a typical childhood of her time, and that at age 11 she disappeared." Ms. Nicholas's face was stern but I could see a glint of inquiry in her eye. I knew better, though, than to open my mouth lest everything I already knew spill out.

Fortunately, Mariah queried so I didn't have to. "You said *disappeared*, not *died*?"

"I did," Ms. Nicholas said. "I can find no record of Lily Sumner's death in 1980 or any year thereafter. Until I can, I will think of her as having disappeared since that is the more accurate term in this situation."

"You think she was kidnapped," Mark said with a bit of alarm.

"I don't think anything," Ms. Nicholas replied. "I only know that according to any form of public record, the young woman disappeared in 1980, at just around the date on that gravestone. Beyond that date, I know nothing."

I couldn't help but notice that Ms. Nicholas didn't mention the allegations Lily hinted at in her journal, but given the nature of our conversation here, I decided to leave that be and hoped Mariah and Mark would follow my lead. It felt important not to clue Linda and Rob into how much we knew.

"Did you find anything about Simon Sumner?" I asked.

Ms. Nicholas raised an eyebrow. "That, while not necessarily more interesting, is at least the more substantive story as far as archival records," she said as she pulled a thin stack of papers out of her briefcase.

"Simon Llewelyn Sumner was born on November 11, 1856 and died eight days later. According to the small mention I found of him in the family papers at the society, he was interred here on the property, presumably just where his grave lies." She gestured behind herself toward the boxwood room. "What is interesting is the reason for his death."

Now, it was my turn to raise an eyebrow. "Oh?" I said.

"Indeed," Ms. Nicholas continued. "His mother's journal

indicates he smothered under a blanket in the wee hours of the morning. But his older sister's journal suggest that perhaps his mother had more to do with his death than her own recollections allow."

Mariah put a hand to her mouth. "His sister thought their mother killed him."

"Sadly, I'm afraid so. She says, and I quote, 'Mother had grown quite fierce with Baby over the past few days given his colic and his cries. I fear she may have silenced him with more than soothing tonight.'" Ms. Nicholas set the piece of paper she'd been reading from back down in front of her. "She gives no proof of such a thing, and of course, no autopsy was performed on the child. But given what we have gathered of Mrs. Sumner's mental health—"

"Stop it," Rob shouted. "I will not let you disparage her that way. She is, I mean she was a fine woman." He had stood up and was now astride the picnic bench with his hands in fists by his side. "She did not kill her child."

Linda had gone ashen under her red hair, and I thought she might cry. Instead, she took a deep breath and pulled Rob back down to his seat. "He's right. Mrs. Sumner was not a murderer, particularly not a murderer of her own child."

I shot Santiago a quick glance, and he shook his head. Clearly, he was as stunned as I was by this level of confidence from our guests. From the looks on Mark, Mariah, and Ms. Nicholas's faces, they seemed to be puzzled, too. "You two talk as if you knew her. How can you be so certain?"

Linda put her hand on Rob's arm as he started to speak, and he quickly closed his lips again. "We can't, of course. Eliza Sumner lived long before our time, but we have heard the rumors about her many times before, and they have never panned out. She simply was incapable of such an act."

Something about the way Linda spoke reminded me of a movie I'd seen as a kid, where the housekeeper and butler at an old mansion turn out to be ghosts who have lived on the property for over 200 years. It takes the family who has just bought the house a while to figure out what was so odd about the couple, and only when the children stumble onto an old graveyard and see the couple's headstones do they figure out the truth. Linda and Rob looked far too grounded in the twenty-first century to have been alive for hundreds of years, but the way they were talking was definitely giving me the heebie-jeebies.

"How do you know though?" I asked, trying to let my sympathy for Mrs. Sumner come through in my town. "Postpartum depression is a horrible illness that leads women to do the most terrible of things. Isn't it possible that Mrs. Sumner suffered with this illness and did the only thing she knew to do to survive?"

"No," Rob said, slamming his fist down on the table and rattling our tea glasses. "I'm done with this conversation." He stormed off around the house again, and I could almost feel the heat of his anger leaving a trail behind him.

"You have to understand," Linda said as she stood, "We have worked for the Sumner family for a long time, and our parents and grandparents before us. Our loyalties are deep, and it's quite painful to hear any one of them disparaged this way."

I reached up and took her arm. "Please know that none of us is judging Eliza Sumner. We're just trying to get to the heart of what happened here, to find the truth for everyone's sake."

Linda shook off my hand. "I understand that, but sometimes, the truth does not set us all free, you know." Then she stormed off in Rob's wake, leaving me shaken in a way I couldn't quite describe.

"Wow," Mark said as he poured each of us another glass of tea. "What was that all about?"

Santi shook his head. "I've seen loyalty before, but that goes above and beyond the course. These people have been dead almost 150 years. Why get so worked up?"

I sighed. "We've seen it before, though, right? People think it's their job to protect their ancestors' reputations. Happens all the time with people whose great-great-grandparents owned slaves. They try to either distance themselves from what their ancestors did, or they become apologists for slavery. Personally, I think that's why so many Southerners are invested in the "good and glory" legends of the Confederacy. If the Confederacy was fighting for something good, then their ancestors can't have been all that bad. It makes sense, even if it's still very wrong-headed."

Ms. Nicholas nodded. "It does, and that could be part of what is happening here. But did you hear them both refer to Mrs. Sumner as if she was still alive. It's as if they know her, or at least think they do. I believe this will be my next avenue of inquiry – to figure out as much as I can about Eliza Sumner." She stood and carefully placed her papers back into her briefcase. "Thank you for the tea and cake. It was lovely. I will be in touch." With that, she turned, walked to her car, and made her way slowly out the long drive.

I put my head down on the picnic table and sighed. "Why is nothing about history ever easy? I mean it's all over, so why does everyone get so worked up?"

Santiago rubbed small circles on my back as he chuckled. "Maybe just think about what you said, sweetheart."

I glanced over my shoulder. "What?! I only get worked up over awesome things like great finnials or people who do amazingly kind things that no one knows about." I smiled. "I certainly don't need to defend people who did horrible things." I spun around. "I don't do that, do i?"

"Of course not," my fiancé said. "I just thought you might take issue if someone said you shouldn't get so excited about the past."

I cleared my throat as I looked up at Mark and Mariah who were both suddenly very busy with tidying the table cloth. "You may have a point." I leaned back against Santi's torso. "But didn't you all think their reaction was odd?"

"Oh definitely," Mariah said. "They're hiding something, but it's really hard to tell what it is. It doesn't," she glanced over at Mark, "make me feel great about having them around here." She looked around until I saw her eyes fix on Wyatt and his nanny playing in the fields below the house. "Where is Sawyer today?" she asked by way of what was clearly a change in subject.

"Day camp. He goes once a week to this rock climbing gym over in Richmond. His grandmother takes him and hangs out for the day. They both love it." I looked from her to Mark. "If Wyatt wants to go next week, I can see if they have spaces."

"Ooh, he'd love that," Mark said. "Let us know."

The four of us cleared the table and made our way inside, where even the slightly underperforming air conditioning felt great compared to the sauna that was outside. After we deposited the food in the kitchen, the four of us returned to the dining room with fresh glasses of tea.

"Well, we did have a new development in things this morning," Santi said after the four of us were seated around the table. He explained to our hosts about Bourne's visit to him and then to me and then said, "You don't have any problem with Paisley writing about Lily Sumner, do you?"

They both shook their heads. "Why would we? Sounds like a great story, and unlike our compadres from earlier, we do believe the truth will set us free. How can we help?" Mariah said.

"You've already helped so much by letting me look through the attic and all the other materials here in the house," I looked over at Santiago and grinned. "But there is one piece of all this story that I have not let you all in on yet."

"Ooh, what is it?" Mariah asked as she leaned forward. "Is there a secret passage in the house or something?"

"Dagnabbit," I shouted as I slumped back against the chair. "How did you know?"

"You're kidding," Mark said, looking from me to Santiago. "There is not a secret passageway in this house."

"I didn't know," Mariah said as she grabbed my hand when I sat forward again. "I was just teasing. Tell me."

"You're serious, Pais?" Santi asked as we instinctively huddled together around one end of the table.

"I am," I said and lifted my messenger bag to the table where I slipped a hand-drawn sketch of the house's architecture from the front pocket. "Lily drew this for me and said she hoped I would enjoy my Nancy Drew moment." I tapped the corner of the room in which we were sitting on the drawing. "It starts here."

The four of us turned to the built-in shelves that lined the east side of the dining room and stared. To me, everything looked plumb and flush, like any other wall, but according to Lily, if we pushed down on the third shelf from the top, we'd find a secret passage that ran the width of the house and included a narrow stairwell to the upper floors. "Lily said the slaves used to use it to move around the house unseen."

We all sat quietly for a minute, and then Mark practically leaped across the floor and pushed down on the shelf. Sure enough, like it had been opened just minutes earlier, the wall swung open, and behind it, we saw a very narrow, brick-lined hallway.

I squealed in delight but had the foresight to let Mariah get ahead of me as the four of us squeezed into the passageway and began to inch our way along. As soon as we were a few feet from the doorway it began to grow very dark, and we each dug out our phones and turned on the flashlight apps. The space got much brighter, but it was also the light that let me realize just how tight the space was. I couldn't imagine trying to carry anything at all through the space, let alone whatever I needed to deliver or dispatch *and* a candle.

A dozen or so feet further on, the tiny space got even narrower as a wooden staircase rose up the wall on my left. By some sort of silent agreement, the four of us continued on past the stairs, my shoulders now touching both sides of the passage, and made our way a couple dozen more feet to the end, where a small wooden handle was tucked against a stud. When Mark pulled it, the wall swung open, this time into the wine cellar at the other side of the basement.

"I can just imagine enslaved people bustling back and forth to discreetly get more wine for dinner," I said. I didn't add that they'd probably carried bed pans and all kinds of other nasty things down this corridor, but that was surely the case. "I wonder if they found it kind of strange like we do."

Santi shrugged. "Maybe a little at first, but it's tiny in there." He poked his head back around the wall. "Surprisingly, though, it's not full of spiderwebs and snakes."

I nodded, realizing that he was right. "That's true. That's weird, right? In my house, I can just not go into a room for twelve hours and see new spiderwebs. Why aren't there any in there?"

Mark and Mariah shook their heads. "No idea. We didn't even know it existed, so we hadn't told our house cleaners to tend it. We will now, though," Mark said.

"Want to explore the rest?" Mariah said as she winked and slipped back into the passageway with me close at her heels.

"You women go ahead," Mark said. "I think it's time for Santi and me to have a beer."

"Excellent plan," Santi said, and I heard them moving back across the open part of the house toward the kitchen.

"What was Nancy Drew's sidekick's name?" Mariah asked as we shuffled back to and then up the staircase.

"She actually had two," I said, "Bess and George. If I may, I'd say you're more a Bess than a George."

"Oh, and why is that?" Mariah said with a laugh.

"Makeup," I said matter-of-factly. "George wasn't much into makeup if I'm remembering correctly."

Mariah laughed again. "Then Bess, I'll be Nancy!" She stopped at the end of the house above the dining room. "This passageway is really clean, too, and the stairs weren't even rickety. I have nary a cobweb in my coiffed hair," she said in the formal voice of 1950s sitcoms.

I laughed. "Yeah, it's weird. Maybe someone on your staff does know about it and assumed you did?"

She shrugged. "It's possible, I guess." She pulled a handle like the one downstairs, and the door swung open into the bedroom across from the wardrobe where I'd first begun going through papers. "Wow. Now that's kind of creepy. I think we may have to find a way to lock the entrances into bedrooms so that our guests don't get freaked out by the possibility of unexpected guests walking through walls."

"When you put it like that, I'd definitely lock them." I looked back down the passage. "Let's keep going."

"Yes, let's," she said, and swung the wall shut behind her.

We found the entrance to the other bedroom on that floor and then into two more on the third floor, but it was the small door that opened into the attic that really captured our imagination because, tacked to the inside of it, were newspaper clippings. In fact, that whole section of the passageway was covered in articles, all about the Sumner family.

"I guess I know where I'll be tomorrow," I said as I shone my flashlight on some of the articles and saw dates like 1917 and 1883. "If you don't mind, I mean."

"Of course not. I think we'll probably want to keep the articles up. It's kind of quirky that someone preserved them in this secret space, isn't it?" She ran her fingers over the crinkly newsprint.

"Very quirky," I said. "But it had to be more than one person." I pointed to an article from 1832 and then to another from 1989. "These articles span more than 150 years."

Mariah frowned. "The stories about this place keep getting odder and odder. Somehow I imagine Linda and Rob might know about this, given how they were talking today. But I'm not much inclined to ask them."

"I know what you mean. I wouldn't want to ask them either." I studied a couple more articles pasted to the ceiling above us. "Let me see what I can find out before we go asking any questions, okay?"

"I like that plan," she said. "Now, if it's all right with you, let's get out of this tiny hall and back down to the AC."

"Yes, please," I said as I ducked to follow her through the door into the attic and then back down the main staircase to the dining room. The guys were sipping their beers and talking about their favorite fishing holes, and when we sat down to join them, Mariah winked at me, a signal I took as to mean, Let's keep those articles between only us, okay?"

I was quite happy to oblige.

WHEN SANTIAGO DROPPED me off at home that evening before he headed into town for his monthly stint calling Bingo at the fire hall, I poured myself a glass of white wine, grabbed my laptop, and headed to the front porch where the ceiling fan kept things just cool enough for me to enjoy the outside. I had about an hour before Sawyer was home from his 'Baba day' in Richmond, and I wanted to make the most of the quiet.

I had no idea how to begin making sense of anything we'd learned about the Sumner family history today, so I decided I'd go with what I knew – facts. I started a spreadsheet that I entitled "The Sumner Help" and began entering each and every name and the associated dates for the people I knew had once - or still did - work for the Sumners or at their house. After putting down Linda's and Rob's names and their approximate birth dates, based entirely on my own estimation, I culled through Lily's early diary for names of servants and then went through Eliza's materials for the same.

Soon, I had a list of about ten people, including Rob Ford, Sr., the father of the Rob I knew. But that wasn't going to get me very far, so I went into the newspaper database and pulled all the Sumner articles I could find as far back as I could go. I clipped each article and saved it as I read it, noting the names and dates from the articles as I went.

It very quickly became clear that the same families had worked for the Sumners for generations. That wasn't an odd discovery at all, not in a rural place like Octonia, but to realize that these families were Linda's and Rob's ancestors was a bit jarring, especially since neither of them mentioned that long tie to the Sumner family or their house when we talked.

As soon as I had pulled enough data to confirm that, by and large, the only people who had worked for the Sumners were the Robertses, Linda's ancestors, and the Fords, Rob's people, I switched from newspaper research to genealogy. Within a few minutes, I had each of their family lines sketched back about two hundred years, and while I ran out of time to do a name-by-name check against the newspaper articles, I recognized enough first names to be sure that a lot of the people in those trees had worked at the Sumner Place in one role or another. It would take me a little more digging to parse out who did what when, though, and with Sawyer due home, I didn't want to start something I could not finish.

I shot Santiago a quick text, packed up my research tools, and made popcorn. Saw would be tired when he got home, but a little popcorn and a short show would give us a chance to talk and connect before he went to bed.

It would also give me a moment to settle in with what I'd found and let my mind begin to puzzle out exactly what this long series of family relationships meant for Ms. Nicholas's theory that Eliza Sumner had killed her child. And, I wondered, what it meant for why Lily had run away.

7

By mutual agreement, Santi and I had decided to take a night off from everything when he got home from bingo, so we had watched the first episode of *Eureka*, an older sci-fi show that was fun and a little ridiculous before we'd crawled into bed early.

Unfortunately, I still didn't sleep well. My dreams were full of time travel episodes that included Linda and Rob and a ghostly figure who walked through walls. When I finally pried myself out of bed at 5, I was exhausted, agitated, and desperately in need of coffee.

Fortunately, my fiancé was one of the "take care of things before they need taking care of" people, and the coffee was already set to go when I stumbled into the kitchen. Both he and Sawyer were still sound asleep upstairs, so after I got my coffee, I settled myself at the dining room table with my research again.

It took me almost no time at all to confirm that the Robertses and the Fords had worked for the Sumner family for at least eight generations back. From what I could gather, a

Roberts had been the heads groundskeeper since the early eighteenth century with a Ford in the role of overseer for everyone who worked on and in the house. It seemed the previous generation trained their replacements, passing the trade and position on to their offspring, who had, until the past couple of decades, notably been only male.

That bit of detail confirmed, I let myself follow a bit of a hunch and looked at the men in both families who were working at the Sumner house when Lily's abuse had begun. From what I had gathered in both her journals, the person had been significantly older than her, but still young enough that a pre-teen girl could label him "cute." From absolutely no scientific process, I decided that put him between 20 and 30.

It became quickly apparent that the only worker who fit that age-range was Linda's father, Felix, and the few bits of information I had about him gave no indication that he was anything but a stellar groundsman and good citizen. Of course, people were not always what they appeared, but that possibility was at a dead end as far as the information I had available, so I let it go.

As I fixed myself a second cup of coffee, I wrestled with my guilt about directly defying Lily's wishes by trying to identify her abuser. I wasn't about to share anything I'd found with anyone besides Santiago, and now that I'd pretty well determined that the abuse wasn't linked to whatever strange secret Linda and Rob were keeping, I didn't feel like I needed to pursue my research in that direction any more. But that didn't mean I wasn't curious.

Crap, I was curious about everything. That's what made me good at my job, and it's also what got me into a lot of trouble.

So for the sake of Lily and my own safety, I decided to begin writing up my article about her experience so that I could include it in my next email newsletter. It wasn't my usual sort of piece, but since Mark and Mariah didn't mind that it would be tied to their place, I figured I could work some elements about the house – including the strange boxwood room and the gravestones – into the article, too. I was saving the story about the secret passageway until next week because it deserved its own write-up, but I did talk about the papers, the donation to the historical society, and the beautiful wardrobe that I now had for sale in my shop.

Primarily, the piece was crafted around Lily's own words. I pulled quotes generously from both her journals, and when I was finished, the article read as part historical memoir and part editorial about the dangers women have always faced from a world that doesn't believe them or consider them as valuable as the men around them. It was, by far, the most controversial piece I'd ever written, but it also felt, in some ways, like my most honest piece, too.

Before I could second-guess myself, I copied it into my email program and sent it out, following up with a quick email to Bourne and then to Mark and Mariah. They needed a heads up that they might get some questions.

It felt like a relief to have that work done and in the world, and I also knew, without a doubt, that there'd be some blow-back. But at that moment, I felt good, proud of what I'd done and hopeful that Lily felt the same. I'd been very careful to not mention anything identifiable about where she was now, even as I talked about her vast philanthropic and entrepreneurial success, and I could only wait to hear her response when and if she wanted to send one.

By that time, it was almost 7, and I could hear the guys stirring upstairs, so I put on a fresh pot of coffee, made some eggs in a basket for all of us, and even cooked up an entire pound of bacon to fuel us for our day. I had a feeling it was going to be a doozy.

As we packed up the house, I stared longingly at my cross-stitch basket and the brand new Lily linen I'd bought to begin a new blackwork sampler. Sawyer was about to go away with his dad for a few days, and that project and I had some long hours ahead of us. I missed sewing, but of late, I hadn't had much time to pick up the needle. That needed to change.

BUT NOT AT THE MOMENT. I was headed back to the Sumners to explore some more closets and drawers with Mariah. She felt confident we'd gotten the bulk of the small stuff with the wardrobe and the attic, but before we began deciding what furniture I'd take and what they'd keep, she wanted to be sure we sorted all the nooks and crannies for any remaining "littles."

Since those littles were my bread and butter, I didn't object at all. Besides, the nosy woman in me was eager to do what I always wanted to do in other people's houses – wade through the accumulation of lives that gathered in long-forgotten drawers.

Santi dropped us off at the big house with a promise to be back with lunch, and Sawyer took off around the side of the building as soon as he caught sight of Wyatt and what appeared to be a quite beleaguered kitten. Our own cat Beauregard was not loving all this time we were spending away from home, but if he knew that coming out with us might involve two preschool boys and all their attention, he'd be glad to be curled on his blanket on the couch in our quiet house.

With a quick rap on the front door, I let myself into the front room of the Sumner house and took a deep breath. Old air just had a certain smell, a smell I loved. I knew it was probably mold spores and mildew, and when I was hooked to oxygen in my old age I might regret my affinity for that scene, but right now, I savored it as I moved toward the big antique desk in the corner of the room as Mariah and I had planned by text a bit ago.

She was finishing up an online call and had told me to go ahead and get started. I had to say I didn't mind one bit because desks were amazing things. Even going through my own brought up a series of memories, usually inspired by the pens I'd used during various stages of my life. Recently, I'd unearthed a whole collection of those pencils with multiple tips that I'd used in elementary school. They were even the neon colors that had been so popular at the time, and seeing them had swept me right back to Ms. Mackey's fifth-grade math class and all the logic problems she'd had us do.

I didn't see any neon when I opened the large, slatted wooden front on the desk, but I did see papers. Lots and lots of papers shoved into every little cubby of that beautiful wood. Without much thought, I grabbed the tufted ottoman from the nearby armchair and set it by the desk chair into which I lowered myself. Then, I began to sort.

Mostly, the papers were various receipts for stuff related to the household and farm. I loved seeing the old blueprint from those sliding credit card machines, and I smiled at a report card from the 1980s for some Sumner child who excelled at PE but not at much else. All of these things were pretty useless as objects themselves, but I knew that Ms. Nicholas would probably still like to sort through them for future displays at the historical society.

I had made it through most of the open part of the desk and was just about to begin searching through the drawers when I heard a screeching yell from just above me and then the sound of crying and pounding feet. I stood up and ran toward the staircase, afraid someone had gotten hurt. As I sprinted up the stairs, I was met by the tiny bodies of two boys, both with tears streaming down their faces. I pulled them close to me and was just about to ask them what had happened when the source of the screeching came to the top of the stairs.

There was Linda, her hair wild, and her mouth open with what was surely going to be another shout. But when she saw me, she slapped her mouth shut and stood with her hands on her hips, lording over me and the two shaking boys.

"What is going on here?" I said, trying to keep my voice steady even as I felt my temper rising. I looked at Linda, but when she simply scowled back at me, I turned to my son. "Saw, are you okay?"

He shook his head. "She scared me," he whispered.

I pulled the boys against my hips as I stood up and glared at Linda. "What happened?"

Linda looked like she was about to walk away without answering me, but I took a step up toward her, the boys still at my side, and asked again, this time with the full wrath of a woman who saw the fear in the eyes of a child she loved. "What happened, Linda?"

The woman straightened her spine and said, "They should not be playing in there. It is not appropriate."

If I hadn't been so very angry I might have laughed. Clearly this woman had not spent much time with preschoolers, who literally and figuratively had no idea about even the concept of appropriate. "Playing where?" I hissed.

"We found a secret tunnel," Wyatt said from somewhere around my left knee.

"You did?" I said as I smiled down at him. "How fun." My smile fell away as I looked up at Linda. "So what? They were playing in the secret passageway. Big deal."

Linda's face went white and even colder. "You know about the passageway?"

At that moment, Mariah walked in, and her quick glance at the situation must have given her a good read on things because she put down the tray of iced tea she was holding and said, "Paisley, what is happening here?"

The fact that she asked me, her new employee, and not Linda, the employee of generations, felt telling, and I saw Linda's jaw grow tight.

I looked over at Mariah again and said, "The boys were playing in the secret passageway," I took a deep breath, "and Linda was concerned."

Mariah's gaze shifted over to the other woman. "Mark and I checked all the tunnels last night. I didn't see anything dangerous. Is there something we should know?" Her tone was casual, but I could see the heavier question in her eyes. I was sure Linda could see it, too.

Linda's shoulders raised and then lowered as she let out a long slow stream of air. "I didn't realize you all had found the passageways. But I'm glad you have. Rob and I have been keeping that secret to ourselves for far too long."

I looked from Linda to Mariah as I tried to get a read on this bit of information. Somehow, it felt like a relief to hear Linda admit they'd been hiding them, but it also brought up a ton of questions about why. It wasn't my place to ask all my questions, though, so I waited, rubbing the heads of the two little boys still huddled beside me.

"Why did you think you needed to keep them a secret?" Mariah asked. "We own this house. You didn't think we had a right to know?"

Linda looked at the boys and then knelt down. "I'm sorry, boys. I didn't mean to scare you." She stood back up. "Can I show you something?" She was still looking at them, but they didn't respond.

"We'll go with you," I said down to Wyatt and Sawyer. "Besides, don't you want to see it again?"

The boys looked at each other and then up at me to nod.

The shimmer in their eyes told me they were both feeling more safe now.

"Let's go then," Mariah said.

Linda led us back into the dining room and then popped open the passageway door there. "The tunnels are really fun, and if it's okay with Mrs. Owen, they're totally good to play in. But you need to know what to do if one of the doors gets locked from the outside."

My heart sped a bit. "It's possible to get locked in there."

Linda nodded, and something about the somberness of her face suggested I shouldn't ask why they were built that way in front of the kids. She reached up to the very top shelf of the door and pushed down on the edge. I heard a faint click. "Now, it's locked," she said.

I looked over at Mariah, and her eyes were wide. "Okay, so what happens if we're inside and need to unlock it."

Linda motioned us all into the passageway behind her, and then gestured for Mariah to pull the door shut.

My boss hesitated just a second before pulling the door too, and I certainly hoped the other doors weren't locked as well. We moved down the dark hallway, and the boys gripped my hands tightly. Given their giggles, I figured they were probably more excited than scared, but since I was a little scared myself, I held tight to their tiny fingers.

Linda led us up the narrow staircase and partially down the hall toward the back of the house. There, she knelt down, flipped something up with her hand, and then pushed. A low opening in the wall appeared, and she crawled through it, followed closely by the boys.

When I made my way out, I saw we were in the bedroom with the wardrobe. We had crawled out through the fireplace. The coal burning insert had swung up to let us through.

"Some ingenious slave—workers," Linda said, "put in this fail safe."

"Slaves built this," Sawyer said. "How awesome."

I smiled. I had begun teaching my boy the actual facts of history from day one, and he didn't shy away from the truth, even when it was hard.

"That is awesome," I said. "And maybe necessary?" I wasn't going to ask more details, but I couldn't hold back that bit of curiosity.

"Yes," Linda said and left it at that. "Let me show you all how to open it just in case."

AFTER OUR LESSON on the fireplace, we let the boys go back to their explorations, this time with flashlights, and Linda showed us how the locking mechanism worked. "The original Sumners had felt it necessary to, on occasion, lock the people they enslaved into the passage as punishment."

I shivered. "As punishment?"

"More as insurance that they were there when the Sumners wanted them." Linda shook her head. "Pretty awful."

"Is that why you were keeping the passageways a secret? Because of the hard history associated with them?" Mariah asked.

"No," Linda said as she sunk down on one of the dining room chairs. "I don't really know why we didn't tell you. Just force of habit, I guess. We've just been keeping the secret for so long."

"But why? Whose secret was it? Were the Sumners ashamed of their family's history?" I'd worked with enough families who had enslaved people in the past to know that the shame and guilt were big for some people.

Linda sighed. "No. I mean, yes," she said quietly, "but it was more about recent history."

I felt a chill pass over me.

Mariah glanced at me and then back at Linda. "What do you mean?"

For a minute, I thought Linda wasn't going to say anything. She kept opening her mouth and then closing it again. Finally, though, she said, "About fifty years ago, one of the family members, well, let's just say he behaved very badly, and he used these tunnels to do some awful things."

That chill sank into my bones. "You're talking about the man who abused Lily."

Linda cut her eyes to me and nodded. "I read your article. As far as I know, you got the facts right." She studied my face. "What I don't know is how you knew all that."

Mariah waved a hand. "Never mind that." She sounded peeved, and I couldn't blame her. This was a lot of secrecy and ugliness to manage in one's new house. "Who was the man?"

"I can't say." Linda's face was pale, and she looked exhausted.

"Are you serious?" Mariah raised her voice. "You're going to protect a child molester?"

I put my hand on Mariah's arm. "She made a promise to Lily."

Linda's shoulders sagged. "I did. We all did."

Mariah's eyes jumped from Linda to me. "She didn't want him prosecuted?"

"It's complicated," Linda said. "I can't say more, but let's just say that we all understood."

I certainly didn't understand, but since I had made Lily the same promise, by proxy, I wasn't in much of a position to judge.

Mariah shook her head and then walked out of the room. For a moment, I thought she might have just left, decided to get some air or something, but she quickly came back with the tray of iced tea and set it on the table.

"Seems like we might need to catch up on quite a few

things. Paisley, do you mind if we put off going through drawers?" Mariah set a glass in front of each of us and poured.

"Not at all. Do you want me to stay? I can head out." Of course, I really wanted to stay, and while this history had consumed me as much as anyone for the past few days, it wasn't really any of my business what Linda knew, unless Mariah wanted me to know it.

"No, please stay," Mariah said and then looked over at Linda. "I'd like her to know everything, if that's okay with you."

Linda studied my face a minute then gave a crisp nod. "Okay. Seems like you know a fair amount already."

I couldn't read her tone. Resigned? Annoyed? Maybe some of both? "I spoke with Bourne a couple of days ago."

Something in Linda's expression relaxed. "She's been in touch with you then."

I nodded, and Mariah looked puzzled. "Who?"

"Lily," I said and explained about meeting her moderator. "But I don't know the name she uses now, and I don't need to know."

"Good." Linda took a long sip of her tea. "The surviving Sumners do not know where Lily is or anything about her, and for reasons I'm about to explain, it's important they not ever know."

Mariah and I nodded and sat back to listen.

After another sip of tea, Linda began. "When Lily was 9, a member of the family began to abuse her. Her parents chose to discount what she told them as exaggeration, but my mother, Lily's caretaker, believed her. Between what Lily said and what some of the other help around the house had seen, the staff knew that this man was dangerous and that Lily was going to continue to be in danger."

Again, a zillion questions zinged through my mind, but I let them dance while Linda continued to talk.

"Rob's father and my dad put together a plan to protect the

girl. The idea was that someone would stay with her every night, sleeping in her room. And during the day, it was easy enough to make sure she wasn't alone," Linda said. "But the man got suspicious after a few days when he couldn't get to her, apparently. One night, my dad saw him putting Lily's pink suitcase into the trunk of his car and got worried that she might be kidnapped."

Mariah's hand clenched on the table. "What did he do?"

"He and Rob's father got her out." Linda's voice was matter-of-fact, as if people helped children escape abusive relatives on the regular.

"Wow," I whispered. Then a question occurred to me. "They told her parents she had died? Is that why there was a tombstone?"

"Exactly. Dad told them he found the bandanna she always wore down by the river with her shoes, said he thought she'd gone swimming and drowned." Linda shook her head. "He didn't think they really believed him, but they didn't ask any questions. Just had a small ceremony and put in that stone."

"And no one asked where Lily had gone?" I asked.

Linda shook her head. "If they did, her parents just said they'd decided to send her to school up north. It was a sort of community deception. Everyone knew something was wrong, but no one said anything."

A year or two earlier, I would have been dumbfounded by this kind of community delusion and secrecy, but given all the research I'd done into Octonia's past, I'd learned that nothing shocked me anymore. Horrified me, yes, but didn't shock me.

"So that's why there weren't any newspaper stories about her death or disappearance?" I asked. "It was a cover-up."

"Was and still is," Linda said. "I have to ask you, for Lily's sake, not to tell anyone about what I've just told you."

"Surely, though, the man who did this to her is dead," Mariah asked. "This was almost forty-five years ago, right?"

"Yes, it was a long time ago," Linda said.

I didn't say anything, but I did note that she did not say the man was dead. I shivered again. "I won't say anything," I said.

Mariah was silent a minute. "If this is Lily's wish, I won't say anything either. But I am appalled that everyone would just pretend this didn't happen."

"Lily didn't pretend," I said, thinking of all the community work she'd done to protect other children.

"No, no she did not," Linda said. Something like pride rang out in her voice, and I found my entire perception of Linda had changed. She was a woman who had carried a secret her entire life and done so without question. Loyalty was clearly etched deep in her DNA.

I poured myself another glass of tea and held up the pitcher to ask the other women if they wanted some. When they declined, I sat back down and said, "Can you tell me about the baby, about Simon."

Linda smiled sadly. "Oh yes, Simon's death was not a secret. As I understand it, he only lived eight days. His body is actually buried by that stone. I work hard to be sure it's protected, as is Lily's monument. That little room is sort of my sacred space."

"It must have horrified you that I found it, then," I asked.

Linda shook her head. "Worried me, yes, but it didn't horrify me. I've been watching you work with the Sumner family stories. You're respectful but honest. I wish my parents had been able to be the same."

I sighed. "It must have been hard for all of you to carry that secret so long. Probably still is hard."

"It is, but it's worth it," Linda said. She stood to go. "I need to get back to work. Honeysuckle is trying to take over the forsythia, and I will win that battle." She smiled and began to walk toward the door.

"Before you go," I said as I stood too, "can I ask you one last question?"

Linda stopped and gave me that same quick nod. "Okay."

"Did the first Mrs. Sumner kill her husband?"

I had intentionally sprung that question on her out of the blue so that I could see if she was shocked.

She wasn't. Instead she shrugged. "I've always wondered about that." Then, she turned and walked out the door.

8

L inda's cryptic response left me a bit dumbfounded, and I stood staring after her for a few moments before turning to Mariah with a shrug of my own. "One mystery not really solved, another deepened."

"If it wasn't all so completely terrible, these stories would be very exciting. But I'd prefer to go to someone else's house for the murder mystery party, thank you very much." She looked a little pale, and I found myself quite sad that the Owen's purchase of this beautiful house came with so much dark history.

"Want to call it quits for the day? Maybe go see some action movie or something?" I wasn't exactly inviting my boss out for the afternoon, but something with car chases and stereotypical villains getting justice sounded good about now.

"While that does sound lovely, if you're up to it, I'd like to continue our investigation into the drawers. If that's not too much, I mean," she said with a look of concern.

"Not too much at all. Maybe we can pretend we're at someone else's murder mystery party?" I said with a laugh. "I think there are some vintage outfits upstairs if you really want to get in the spirit."

She smiled. "Now you're talking." She turned back to the table. "Let me get us some more tea, and we'll get back to that desk."

WE SPENT the next two hours going through the rest of the desk drawers and the small drawers in the four side tables around the living room. For the most part, we found partially used notebooks of random scribblings, receipts, and a few more photos. Nothing that stood out as particularly important, and not a thing that gave us any more information about Lily's story or whether Mrs. Sumner was a murderer.

The nanny had stopped in to be sure it was okay she feed Sawyer lunch and had asked if she could take the boys to the pond down the hill. After she assured me she'd put both boys in life vests and keep a close eye on them, I told her that was a great idea. Now that I was back in research mode, I was eager to get more done, and if Sawyer was occupied then I had the time and space to do it.

"You up for tackling another room?" I asked Mariah. "Or I can just go in on my own."

She smiled. "I was actually hoping to get out into the garden, so if you're good to go through the library without me, I'll leave you to it."

"Of course," I said, both a bit disappointed not to hang out with this person who was quickly becoming a friend and excited to just move at my own pace with my own systems for a couple of hours.

I headed toward the library and began systematically with the shelves to the right side of the door. Each inch of the walls in this room, with the exception of the tall windows at the back and the doorways, was covered in floor-to-ceiling bookcases, and while most of the shelves were filled with books set spine out, there were also other trinkets tucked into the spaces.

Carefully, I pulled each book from the shelf, and studied it, then logged the title, author, and year, leaving the most fragile and oldest out in a stack on the steamer trunk that served as a coffee table by the soft, well-worn couch across the room.

I also made a collection of items for me to take and sell – an old bugle that I'd have to get dated but that looked quite old, a copper owl that was also a bank, a flashlight with a red signal light at one end and a big search light at the other. All these oddities would do very well in my shop, and they might even be worth enough to put them into an auction house for sale.

By the time I made the turn at the first corner and was inching my way over to the fireplace in the center of the wall, I estimated I had a few hundred dollars' worth of items to sell, and I'd made a decision to bring in a book buyer to evaluate the books because there were so many eighteenth and nineteenth century titles that I thought were probably collectible. This room alone might pay for Sawyer's school tuition for a year. It was exciting.

Outside the long windows at the back of the house, I could see Mariah in her wide-brimmed hat and gloves working away in the fenced vegetable garden. She looked right at home, and I knew just how she felt. There was something simply so wonderful about seeing things you drop in the ground become plants. And if she was anything like me, weeding was its own kind of satisfaction.

I began to study the painting and the small knick-knacks on the mantel over the brick firebox. Here, the previous owners had run a line for gas logs, so I was sure they'd done some work on the chimney and hearth to make them fire-safe. But the fireplace surround itself looked original with its turned legs and plinths under a simple mantel at the top. It was a beautiful piece, and I wondered if Mariah and Mark wanted to keep it.

In the interest of preparation, I began to peek behind the wooden surround to see how it was attached to the fireplace itself. Often, modern construction methods allowed the surround to be screwed right into the rock or stone of the chimney itself. But originally, the structure would have been adhered to the wooden framing around the chimney, which meant it was easily removed with a crowbar.

My quick inspection showed the mantel to be embedded right into the neighboring bookcases, and for a moment, I feared I would have to disassemble the shelves to get it off, should the Owens decide they didn't want it. I thought maybe the shelves themselves could be removed, and so I tugged on the one at the height of my shoulder and to the right of the fireplace.

The plank didn't move outward, but it did click down two inches, and when it did, a narrow box, about two inches wide, slid out from just beside the leg of the surround. Given that the box stood about three feet tall and protruded from the fireplace about eighteen inches, it was a pretty prominent secret storage place. I couldn't see any items down inside, but before I examined them, I wanted to see if there was a matching drawer on the other side.

Sure enough, a matching drawer popped out when I pressed down on the corresponding shelf. I was giddy with excitement, and while I wanted to go get Mariah and show her immediately, I was also really eager to examine what was there without having to share. I reached into the left-side drawer and pulled out three rolls of paper. My heart rate quickened as I carried the tubes to the dining room to spread them out.

Very quickly I saw that they were architectural drawings, old ones, probably the original ones for this house. They were hand-drawn and showed the elevations and room layouts for all three floors of the Sumner Place. I could even see the secret passageways running between the rooms on each floor. These drawings were beautiful.

After setting various glasses and books on the corners to keep them from rolling back up, I went back in to check the first drawer I'd found. I reached all the way to the bottom without finding anything, and then I walked my hand to the far back of the drawer. Just as I was about to decide there was nothing there, my fingers bumped against something jutting out and then rifled the edge of some papers. I carefully gripped the whole lot and lifted them into the light.

I was holding a slim book and several photographs, tintypes specifically. They were beautiful and dusty enough to make me think they had been in that space for quite a long time. I sat down on the couch and carefully looked at each photo. The first showed a somber woman in a black dress with a wide skirt and draping sleeves. Her hair was up and curled carefully around her face, but while it was obvious the styling had taken a long time, spirals of curl and flyaways jutted out and gave the woman a bit of a frenzied appearance.

The second image I looked at showed a man asleep in a four-poster bed. He had spare gray hair that hung just about to his chin, and it looked like he could use a shave. He wore some sort of striped shirt or sleeping gown, and his face was turned just a bit away from the camera.

I moved the image closer to my face and studied it. Something about the man looked a little off. I couldn't put what I was noting into words, but he somehow didn't look right. Then, I gasped. He was dead. I knew it. This was a photo of a dead man, and unlike the other memorial photos we'd found, this image wasn't staged. This man was in the position he'd been when he died, and it was completely creepy.

To keep myself from getting spooked out even more, I put the photo down and turned my gaze to the final item I'd retrieved from the drawer. This one was by far the weirdest and

most disturbing. It featured the woman in the black dress
sitting on the side of the bed next to the dead man. She wasn't
looking at him but instead staring at the camera. The man
could have been a statue in a park for as much as she was
attending to him. The image felt like a memento of sorts, a
really disconcerting memento, like a photograph you'd take
when you visited a famous historical site or something.

But as weird as the woman's pose next to the body was, it
was her face that sent chills across my skin. Her expression was
calm, passive almost, but there, at her mouth, one corner was
turning up in a slight smile. I turned the photo over face down
on the trunk in front of me, as a shiver crept up and down my
spine like a low current.

Finally, and with not a small amount of anxiety, I opened
the slim book I had discovered. It was full of scrawling handwriting that moved across the pages in a slanting scrawl that
grew more and more chaotic with each page. But I was able to
read enough to discover this was another of Mrs. Sumner's
journals, and in this one, there was no doubt she was
confessing to murder.

*My husband has belittled me and my opinions for the final time.
The laurel tincture has been mixed, and I will administer it when I
take up the tea he demands of me each evening. Molly, the maid, has
been informed not to enter his room for any reason, and I will be
sure the passageway is secured before I leave. Tomorrow, I will be
free.*

THE NEXT ENTRY described how she found her husband the
next morning, "striped dressing gown," "placid expression,"
and I knew instantly that the photos were of her and him after
she had murdered him. My hands began to shake.

Quickly, I flipped through the final pages of the journal –
there were many tens of pages total – but almost everything

after those two entries was illegible, the scrawl of a woman who had, seemingly, experienced a psychotic break.

I set the book down next to the photos and took a few deep breaths. Clearly, this was evidence Santi needed to see so that he could finish up his own investigation and close the books on the murder he'd just found out about. But first, I wanted to show Mariah what I'd found.

I walked over to the window and waited until Mariah stood and turned toward me, her arms and shirt piled high with what looked like potatoes. After waving my arms around to get her attention, I motioned for her to come inside, and she gave me a quick nod. I didn't feel comfortable leaving these items for even the few moments it would take me to walk outside and get her. They were too valuable, and something about the fact that they'd been hidden for a long time made me think they might be dangerous, too.

While I waited for Mariah to come in and wash up, I carried the journal and the photos, facing down and away from me, into the dining room and took out my phone to text Santi. I was just about halfway into my message when Mark walked in with a thin, blond man in a cowboy hat behind him. As soon as I saw the man in the hat, I instinctively slid the journal and tintypes under the table and into my lap. Whoever this was didn't need to see them.

"Hi Mark. Look what I found," I said as the men leaned over the table.

"Are these what I think they are?" Mark said as he sat down and peered at the yellowing sheets of paper.

"They appear to be the original drawings for this house," I said with a smile that mirrored Mark's own.

"Where did you find these?" The man with Mark snapped. "I've looked for these for twenty years."

I looked from the man to Mark, and Mark gave me a small nod.

"They were in a secret drawer beside the fireplace in the library," I said quietly, not at all comfortable with sharing more than was necessary with this guy.

"What secret drawer?" Mariah said as she came in from the kitchen while drying her hands on a dishtowel. "You found another secret spot?" She was smiling, but I could see the wrinkle between her brows as she looked at the man peering down at the blueprints.

"I did," I said. "It's pretty cool." I had every intention of showing the Owens both drawers, but I didn't think it was my place to reveal more than necessary to this strange, grumpy man.

Ever more mannerly than I was, Mariah extended her now dry hand to the man and said, "It's good to see you again, Mr. Sumner. This is our friend and consultant Paisley Sutton." She gestured at me and smiled.

The man shook Mariah's hand and then mine with an abrupt downthrust before dropping my fingers like they had burned him. "I saw Ms. Sutton's article this morning, and that's why I'm here. I would really appreciate if you'd quit running my family's name through the mud." His glare set up my hackles, and I imagined that if Beauregard was here, he'd be doing that arched back and hissing thing that always scared the beejezus out of me.

"Pardon?" I said, trying my best to be polite but also being sure the acid I was feeling seeped into my words. I did not like to be accused of gossip or slander, neither of which I was guilty of in this or in any case, for that matter.

"None of what you wrote was true about Lily. No one hurt that girl. She just got too full of herself and then drowned. Bunch of lies you're spreading to defame my family."

Solomon's voice was rigid and full of rage. I was glad I wasn't alone with him, mostly because he seemed angry enough to hurt me but also because, especially after what I'd just found, I was in no mood to be accused of lying. No mood at all.

Mark looked at me, and this time, I shook my head. I didn't need him to step in. I had this one just fine. "Sir, I understand that what I wrote was disturbing and painful to you, obviously, and to members of your family. But I assure you every word was accurate and fact-checked by people who can attest to the truth without a doubt." I was not about to bring Lily into this conversation. I didn't know what Solomon knew, didn't know if he even believed her to be alive, and I wasn't about to put her at risk again just to prove my own credibility.

"Who is your source? I was there when that girl drowned in that very river." He jabbed his finger out toward the back of the house. "You don't know—"

"That's enough, Mr. Sumner," Mark said as he stepped closer to the man. "Unless there's something else we can do for you, I believe it's time for you to go."

Solomon looked up at the larger man's face and took a step back. "No, sir. It's clear that no one in this house is interested in the truth. So we'll take care of the situation ourselves." He tipped his hat in a sort of half cowboy-half insult way and walked out.

My hands were shaking under the table, but I slowly lifted them and the photos and journal out to the top of the table and set them down. I was eager to tell them more, but first I needed a minute to process what had just happened. "Does he seem strangely angry over something that happened four decades ago?"

Mariah nodded. "I mean, I know his family is important to him, but seriously..." She paused and then looked at me. "Unless...."

My stomach plummeted. "Unless...." I slammed against the back of the chair and shook out my shoulders. "How old do you think he was?"

Mark frowned and looked at me before saying, "70 maybe, give or take. Why?"

"Because then he's the right age to be the man Lily wrote about in her journal," Mariah said as she sat down across from me.

At this, Mark dropped into the chair nearest him. "You think he is the one who abused Lily." Mark's voice was almost a whisper, and I couldn't tell if that was because of the shock of what we'd just surmised or because he was worried Solomon was still in the house somewhere.

"I think it's time to get Santi to look into things," I said as I picked my phone back up, finished my initial message, and then added information on Solomon's visit.

"Tell Mark and Mariah I'll be there in fifteen," was his full reply.

I told my hosts and said, "Let me order pizza?" It was already late afternoon, and if the boys had been swimming this whole time, they were going to be exhausted and hungry. Plus, I was exhausted and hungry.

"Actually, Saul is coming over for a barbecue, so let's just plan to have you guys stay, too." Mariah stood up. "I love cooking for a crowd."

"She really does," Mark said. "In fact, why don't you invite Ms. Nicholas over, too? Sounds like we need all the help we can get to figure out what's going on."

"If it's not too much to ask, maybe I can invite my friends Mika and Mary, too. They've helped me out with research in the past, and they know everyone and everything in Octonia." I felt a little awkward inviting people to someone else's house, but Mark was right. We needed help.

"Absolutely," Mariah said as she walked around the table to head for the kitchen.

I stood to follow her into the kitchen and my hand brushed against the tintypes. "Oh, wait. I totally forgot to tell you what else I found." I filled them in on the photos and journal and told them what I thought I'd found – the trophies of a murderer.

"My word this is terrifying," Mariah said as she studied the photos of the Sumners. "She posed with his body."

I shook my head. "She definitely looks unwell, psychologically, but I think this may be more than simple postpartum depression," I said.

"Yeah, this makes it look like a very ill woman lived in this house." He shuddered. "What have we gotten into here?"

I sighed and shook my head. "I don't know, Mark, but it doesn't look good. It just doesn't look good."

WHILE BELINDA HELPED WYATT and Sawyer get cleaned up, Mariah and I peeled and cooked potatoes for a massive potato salad, laid out several packages of hot dogs, and made a platter of hamburger patties, and then laid out all the fixings for burgers and dogs. By the time we were finished, the kitchen counter was full of food, all ready to be scooped up buffet-style once Mark finished grilling.

Santi arrived first and helped Mark carry everything out to the grill to get cooking. Mika arrived soon after with a massive pitcher of something I thought, at first, was suntea with mint but turned out to be sangria... with mint. Mariah and I poured big glasses for the three of us and then added a fourth and a fifth when Mary and then Ms. Nicholas arrived. Santi and Mark, like Saul who came soon after, opted for bottles of beer, and soon the kids had drink pouches and the adults had our beverages, so we gathered around the grill and giant firepit by the garden.

If we hadn't been there to talk about murders and assault, it would have been a lovely evening for a barbecue. The air wasn't as humid as it had been, and a nice breeze was coming up off the river. Even the mosquitoes and gnats seemed to have floated elsewhere for the evening.

But despite our attempts at small talk and casual conversation, the mood was somber. Eventually, when Belinda graciously offered to take the boys into the woods to get sticks for marshmallows, Mark started the more serious part of the conversation. "I don't know exactly what everyone knows, but we've found – Paisley has found – some serious information that we need to discuss how to handle. Paisley, do you mind catching everyone up?"

I didn't mind at all, but my mind was spinning with information and not a small amount of fear. It took me a minute and a bit more sangria to get my head straight. "So, we found two tombstones last week," I began. From there, I told them about Bourne's visit to my store, keeping quiet on the details of Lily's whereabouts and work, then about what I'd found out about baby Simon. Finally, I showed everyone the journal and photographs that I'd brought out in my bag when we moved outside.

My friends carefully passed the items around the circle of camping chairs we'd assembled by the firepit, and in turn, each one of them shuddered before handing the items to the person beside them.

Finally, after a long silence where we all, I assumed, absorbed what we'd just seen, Saul said, "Well, I'll be damned. That woman was gloating over killing a man."

Something about those words in Saul's deep mountain accent got me tickled, and I found that I couldn't hold back the giggle that escaped my lips. Apparently, I wasn't alone, though, because soon everyone was laughing and slapping their thighs, and just like that, the heaviness of the night lifted. We all knew we had to talk about a murder, maybe two, and the fact that a young girl had needed to flee for her own safety. But at this moment, we were together and we were all safe, even Lily.

Somehow, our laughter brought that all into perspective for me. It was going to be okay.

The boys came back just then with about a dozen marshmallow sticks, so we all shifted our attention to grilling marshmallows and making s'mores. I ate two s'mores and four extra marshmallows, and I was fairly sure that my stomach would explode. But it was such a perfect summer night, circumstances of history aside, and I didn't really care.

Eventually, the boys went off to gather lightning bugs, and we returned to our conversation. "Santiago," I said, "is there anything that can be done about the murder of Mr. Sumner?" I wasn't sure exactly what I was asking, but a man had been killed and it seemed wrong, somehow, to dismiss that even though it had happened almost two centuries ago.

Santi nodded and looked into the fire. "Nothing I can do. The murderer is long dead, and anyone who helped her has passed decades ago. But I will write up a full report, and maybe, Paisley, you'd do another article. Give Mr. Sumner a little justice."

I nodded. "As long as that's okay with you," I said as I looked at the Owens. "I don't want to make more trouble for you."

Mark shook his head. "That man makes his own trouble."

"Who?" Mary asked. "What are you talking about?"

Very quickly, Mark told everyone about Solomon Sumner's visit earlier today. "We can't be sure, but we think—"

I interrupted him to keep him from revealing what Lily didn't want anyone to know. "He's obviously very upset, so we think he might try something, maybe something to ruin my reputation."

Santi scowled at me. "You think you're in danger?"

I shook my head. "Not physically, but he did hint that there might be some sort of public step he might take to discredit me." I shrugged. "Let him try."

"You're so brave, Pais," Mika said as she rolled her eyes. "But let's not have too much bravado about threats, shall we?"

I sighed. She was right. I'd had – we'd had – enough danger for a lifetime already. No need to tempt fate, or grumpy men in cowboy hats.

"Well, if I may, can I suggest we do a bit more research into Mrs. Sumner, see if we can't figure out the exact motivation she had for murdering her husband?" She looked over at me. "I'd be happy to contribute some time for your article, Paisley. Perhaps we could publish it in a future issue of the historical society journal, with you running an excerpt, of course, in your own newsletter."

I smiled. "I'd be most grateful for the help, and thank you."

Mary leaned forward. "Let me see if I can get wind of what Sumner is planning. Maybe we can head him off at the pass."

"I like how you think, Ms. Johnson," Saul said. "If I may suggest a partnership in that regard," he stuck out his hand to Mary, who was sitting to his left, and they shook on their new endeavor.

For about the four hundredth time in my life, I felt deep gratitude for my friends' deep care for me, and for the way they stepped in whenever I or anyone else needed them. They were the most generous group of people I'd ever felt, and I counted myself very blessed to have them.

With our plans set and the night growing dark, I decided it was time to bundle my very sleepy little boy into the car and race home before he was completely out. Fortunately, my fears about a car nap were alleviated when Santi offered to give him a ride in the police car with the lights on. That excitement would easily keep him up until we got home.

As they headed that way, I stepped in to help Mariah in the kitchen and realized I'd left quite the mess in the library. "I'll just clean that up, right quick," I said and moved toward the room.

"You will do no such thing," Mariah said. "All of that can wait until tomorrow, if you're able to come then. If not, it'll be just fine until whenever you return."

"Actually, I can come back tomorrow. Just me though. Sawyer is off to see his dad for a few days." I sighed. It was always bittersweet to have my little boy go away. I relished the time to myself and the ability to focus for long periods, but I missed him something fierce.

"That works well because Wyatt is going to see his mom for a few days, too. But he'll be back later next week if the boys want to hang out again." Mariah smiled wearily, and I wondered if she felt the same way about her nephew as I did my son – a mix of relief and sadness when he left. I expected so.

I turned toward the sink to begin loading the dishwasher when Mariah put her hand on my back. "Please, Paisley, let us do this. Mark and I have a system, and it's our time to catch up after the day. You go home to your boys. We'll see you tomorrow."

I smiled and stayed long enough to help my friends bring everything else in. Then, we all hugged goodbye and caravanned out the long driveway into the quiet night of cricket song.

9

———————

The next morning, Sawyer's dad came by to pick him up since the campground they were going to was out past me. I welcomed the extra time in my pajamas and with my coffee, and after Santiago left for work, I decided to enjoy an hour with my cross-stitch on the front porch.

I picked up my basket and my mug and invited Beauregard to join me on the porch. He followed slowly and then stood below the porch swing meowing until I went back inside, got his velour blanket, and then draped it over the king's throne so he could swing and snooze in complete luxury. How this cat had gotten so spoiled was beyond me, a claim my father would shoot down with a lot of evidence to the contrary.

The linen I'd bought was twenty-two count, and I was glad, once again, that I've finally caved to the needs of my middle-aged body and gotten progressive lenses in my new prescription. The sun was bright on the porch, so it was easy for me to see the holes for my all-black stitches, despite the tiny fabric count.

The pattern was a Celtic-inspired tree of life, a design my mother had loved and had wanted to stitch herself. Given that I had less time to stitch than usual in the summer, it was nice to work with only one thread color and simply make my way through the various swirls and loops of the pattern. By the time I needed to head to the Owen's house, I had gotten a couple hundred stitches in and was eager to come back to it that evening.

When I arrived at the Sumner Place, Mariah and Mark were sitting on the small front porch in matching rocking chairs. They looked the perfect image of summer relaxation, and I was tempted to snap their picture from afar. When I got closer, though, I was glad I had quelled that impulse. They looked downright miserable.

"You okay?" I said as I stepped onto the porch and then sat down facing them at the top of the stairs. "What happened?"

Just then, I heard tires on the gravel behind me and turned to see Santiago's cruiser pulling up, followed by a second car. When both Santi and Savannah stepped out and walked toward us, I felt my heart sink. This couldn't be good, and I said that as someone who loved both of these officers deeply.

"You must have the sound off on your phone?" Santi said as he stepped up and took my hand to help me to my feet.

I scooped my phone out of my back pocket, and sure enough, the ringer was off. I clicked it on and then apologized when I saw the three texts and two calls from my fiancé.

He looked over at Mark. "Have you told her?"

Mark shook his head. "She just arrived, and I was about to let her know."

"Let me know what?" I said looking from man to man. "What is going on?"

"Solomon Sumner has issued a cease and desist letter to Mark and Mariah and, thus, by proxy, to you. He wants you to stop your research." Santi shook his head.

"He hasn't got a legal leg to stand on, and I'm sure his lawyer knows that. But he's hoping to scare you," Savannah added, the anger in her voice palpable. "There is nothing you need to do, Pais." Her dark brown eyes were still soft as she looked at me.

"That's right, and I would never advise you to stop researching. But if he's going to these lengths, we need to be sure we're protecting all of you," Santi added. "Savannah is going to stay on site with you too."

I nodded, well-enough schooled in this type of situation to not try and argue. Besides, Solomon had scared me yesterday, maybe more than I had been willing to admit. "Okay. And you'll be at home tonight?" I said.

"I will. And my new deputy will be stationed here at the end of your driveway overnight, Mark and Mariah." Santiago shook Mark's hand and then kissed me on the cheek before going back down the stairs. "Call if anything at all comes up."

The rest of the day was uneventful. I went over the items that I'd noted as being of interest to me, and Mark and Mariah said I should take them all. They loved seeing the secret drawers, and for that reason and because the fireplace surround was gorgeous, they decided to keep it. I was glad they did. It was perfect in that room.

They'd also decided to have the original drawings of the house framed and hung in the living room, where everyone could see them. They were so excited, in fact, that they'd already taken them to a shop in town to have them custom framed. "I can't wait to see how they look," I said. "They were really amazing."

"I know, and the owner of the shop couldn't believe their condition when I dropped them off. Fortunately, he knows how to handle historic documents with care," Mark said.

I had been thinking along similar lines for the books around me. Many of these were historic first editions, not popular titles really, but important ones, I imagined, in various disciplines. They were the kind of thing I could take to even the larger used bookstores and not have any expectation they'd know what they were looking at. No, these needed to go to experts, and I thought I knew just the people.

After Mark and Mariah headed off to their various activities around the place, I took out my phone and called Blue Whale Books in Charlottesville. The clerk on duty said she'd have the owner call me when she was in, and that she was sure they could come out and give an estimate on the cost. I imagined there was a fee for this service, but I would gladly pay that to have an expert evaluate what was here and help us decide how and if to sell the collection.

I continued to make my way around the room, intermittently testing shelves for more secret compartments as I cataloged the books in the room. It was slow work, but also the kind of work that got rhythmic and relaxing the more I let myself succumb to it. By the time I finished the catalogue, I felt tired but at ease in a way I hadn't for a few days. Plus, I had a full notebook with titles and authors that I was eager to look up myself.

When I packed up the knick-knacks I was taking home for sale in my shop, including a set of bookends that looked like Cistercian monks, I wandered into the kitchen where I could hear Mark and Mariah talking as they prepped food. "Stay for dinner?" Mark asked when I came in.

I smiled and shook my head. "Thank you, but I honestly kind of just want to get home and relax."

They both smiled at me. "Raincheck?" Mariah asked.

"Definitely," I said. "I'm going to head out now. I'll be back in the morning to tackle another room if that's okay with you."

"Perfect. You got everything you wanted from the library?" Mariah asked as she walked me to the door.

"I did." I stopped and looked at her. "But you know, you might think of having an auction house come in and help you sell the things I'm not taking. Some of them, especially the furniture, might be quite valuable."

Mariah nodded. "We've actually been talking about that. We're not trying to make a fortune off anything here, but we do want the pieces to be treated well, which means they have to be valued and sold professionally." She opened the front door for me. "Could we extend your contract and ask you to oversee that process for us?"

I grinned. "Absolutely. I'll do some research on auction houses over the next couple of days, and we can make a plan."

She waved, and I made the short walk with my box of finds to the car. I could see Savannah's patrol car up at the end of the driveway, and when I stopped and rolled down my window, she smiled. "Good day?"

"The best," I said. "Quiet and productive. How about for you?"

"Not productive, but quiet, and that's all I can ask for." She stretched and looked out the window. "My relief should be here soon, and I'm looking forward to a long hot bath."

"Ooh, that sounds lovely," I said. "Hope you don't have to be here tomorrow."

"Happy to do what needs to be done," she said and then waved as I put the car in drive and pulled out onto the main road. Savannah was good people, and she was also smart people. If something fishy was going on at the Sumner Place, she'd know it.

My drive home wasn't long, but my mind was swimming with book titles and price estimates. So I put on some music, The Wailin' Jennys, so I could sing along and slow down. I was singing along to "Wildflowers" and feeling the tension slide from my shoulders when I saw a large black SUV come up close behind me.

I sped up a bit, but the vehicle just kept right on my tail. It wasn't uncommon to have someone tailgate on these two-lane roads, and so I had a regular way of getting people to back off. If speeding up didn't work, I tapped my brakes and slowed way down. Sometimes that got the person to back off, and sometimes they just sped around me. In either case, they weren't going to rear-end me if I had to stop suddenly.

But this person didn't do anything but stay right behind me as I slowed down. I decided that I'd pull into the small gas station up the road to let the person pass. But when I put on my turn signal to pull in, they did too. Now I was getting nervous.

So rather than stop at the station, I made the hard left onto the road just before I got there and then gunned it. If I could put some space between me and this person, I could get to the end of the road and turn into a high school friend's driveway and tuck my car behind their barn while I called Santi.

This truck was clearly determined to stay with me, and it was just as clear that they were from around here because they took the quick s-turns just as fast as I did. That wasn't a maneuver someone who didn't know this road could do without having an accident.

I sped up even more on the straightaway, but just when I thought I might pull away, the SUV matched me and got even closer than before. Then, just as we were about to take the final 90-degree turn by my friend's house, the vehicle crossed the double yellow line and pulled up beside me. The windows were tinted dark, so I couldn't see into the cab. But I could definitely see the SUV moving closer to my door. They were trying to run me off the road.

Fortunately, the side of the road was flat here, and I was able to slide my two passenger-side tires off onto the gravel without losing speed. Then, I slammed on the brakes and spun the car right onto an old logging road that ran by my friends' back pasture. The SUV didn't have time to make the turn and zoomed on down the road.

I didn't dare slow down, though, and I was glad for the

bright afternoon sunlight of summer as I sped over the dirt road, my Subaru finally putting her all-wheel drive suspension to the test. I zipped past the detritus of the logging process that had been completed a couple years back and hoped that they had a cut-through up to the major road that led into town. If they didn't, that SUV could hunt me down and trap me back here away from the road.

Just then, I saw a four-wheeler track veer left off the road, and I followed it, apologizing to my car for the bumps and scratches along the way. Then, I was back at the major road, and I hung a fast right and floored the car up the small hill and into downtown Octonia. I didn't slow down as I passed the school, and I didn't even stop for the light at the intersection. A quick scan told me no one was coming, and I flew down the road and hung a left and then a fast right before parking my car and leaping out of it at the police station.

I was out and sprinting for the back door before I even got the car stopped all the way. I rushed inside and bolted toward Santi's office, where I slammed face first into his shoulders. "Paisley, what's going on?"

My breath was rough and fast, and I couldn't get enough air to form my words fully. "Car. Run. Road."

He steered me toward a chair outside his office, and I dropped into it and put my head between my knees. All I could think was, *thank goodness Sawyer wasn't there*. After a couple of moments, my breath started to slow, and I looked up. "Someone just followed me from the Sumner Place and tried to run me off the road."

My fiancé patted my arms and legs and said, "Are you hurt?"

I shook my head. "Got away on the logging road back by Jay's. I don't think he saw me come here."

He stood and took out his phone. "Savannah, Paisley was just followed from where you are. Hold on." He looked down at me. "Can you describe the car?"

"Black SUV. Dark-tinted windows. One of those license plates with the bear on it." I had wanted to get the license plate number, but I hadn't had time or focus to memorize anything. That was the best I could do.

Santi relayed the information to Savannah, and then he knelt down in front of me again. "What do you want to do now?"

I took a slow, deep breath. "Let's go home."

He helped me to my feet and said, "We'll take my car. Give me your keys, and I'll get your things." He helped me into the passenger seat of his cruiser then jogged over, got the box and my work bag out of my car, made sure it was properly in Park, then locked it up.

As we drove toward home, I recounted exactly what happened to Santi, trying to remember every detail in case it was somehow helpful in locating who had done this. I wanted them arrested, not so much for justice but so I could have some answers. Why did someone want to hurt me?

"Do you think this is what Solomon Sumner meant about taking action?" I asked Santi as he took the last turn onto our road.

He sighed. "I really don't know. Somehow I doubt it. He went the legal route the first time. It's a big jump from a cease and desist letter to attempted murder." I felt him glance over at me as I slumped against the passenger-side window. "Do you have any idea who else might want to hurt you?"

I shrugged. "None. As far as I know, I haven't done anything to make anyone but maybe the Sumners peeved, much less homicidal." The adrenaline was wearing off, and I was feeling beyond weary. I was downright exhausted and near tears. "We'll figure this out, right?"

Santi put his hand over mine on my leg. "Of course, we will, and you're not alone, Pais. We're all here for you. I'm here for you."

For the second time in as many days, I felt warmth and relief at that thought. But still, someone had just tried to kill me, and I wasn't actually sure anyone, even my fiancé the sheriff, could do much about that.

ONCE WE WERE HOME, Santi helped me get settled on the couch with a cup of tea, five potential seasons of *Eureka*, and my cross-stitch. I wanted to ask him if he could grab my laptop from my bag and bring it over, too, but I knew he would frown on that idea. I also knew he was right, and I should take a break.

I cued up my show and picked up my hoop and needle, and I let myself disappear into wacky sci-fi and black stitches. I could hear Santi outside on the front porch making phone calls, calls that I knew were about me and the person who had tried to kill me, but I ignored them. He was doing his job, and I had told him all I could. I needed to rest and let my system calm down.

When I woke up a bit later, my cross-stitch was tucked neatly on the bookshelf next to me, and I had a blanket over my legs. Santi sat at the other end of the couch with his computer, and when I sat up, he closed the screen and looked at me. "Did that help?"

I rubbed my eyes and nodded. "Definitely. But now, I'm starving."

"That's my girl," he said. "Mika is on her way with burgers."

I groaned with anticipation. "And fries with vinegar?"

"And fries with vinegar," he said as he pulled me close to him for a hug. "Comfort food to the max."

I snuggled against his chest and tried to let go of the tension I could feel building back up in my body. "Everything okay?" That was the most understated form of the biggest question, but I knew Santi would get it.

"Yes, Savannah put out a BOLO for the SUV, and our new

deputy is at the Sumner Place for the night." He squeezed me tight. "I, of course, took the terrible job of watching over you."

I smiled, but then my brain caught up with what he said. "So you do think this has something to do with the Sumners?"

He shifted down on the couch a bit and stretched his legs out on the ottoman. "I can't be sure, of course, but I suspect so. Better safe than sorry."

I closed my eyes and listened to his heartbeat for a few moments. "What I don't get is why? I mean, I haven't done anything beyond write that one article."

"I don't know, Pais. People act out for all kinds of reasons." He ran his fingers through my curls. "But we'll figure it out."

A knock at the door interrupted our snuggle, but since it was Mika with burgers, fries, and milkshakes, I welcomed the disruption. I gave my best friend a huge hug after off-loading her delivery, and she held me out and looked at me carefully.

"You're not hurt," she asked.

"Not a scratch," I said. "I am, however, thinking of becoming a road rally racer. You should see my skills."

Mika rolled her eyes. "The only things I want to see right now are these burgers. I got you the spicy barbecue one you love."

My mouth started to water. "And you did bring the vinegar?"

She reached into the pocket of her cardigan and pulled out a bottle of the best malt vinegar around. "Of course."

The three of us descended on the food like cattle on fresh pasture, and I only let myself think about how much more vinegar and salt I needed to counterbalance the sweetness of my vanilla shake. The answer to that was a tremendous amount.

Soon, though, the food was gone, my belly was full, and my brain was beginning to spin. I had never taken my value as a human being that seriously before I had a child, but now that he depended on me, I was incredibly livid that someone had tried to hurt my child by hurting me. Of course, I was scared and angry because of the harm someone intended for me, but that was nothing compared to the fury I felt about potential hurt for my son. "So can we talk about who would have done this?"

I heard the long sigh that slipped out of Santi's mouth, but since he didn't actually object to the conversation, I plowed ahead. "As best I can tell, the Sumners are the best suspects. They already threatened me, and they seem really invested in keeping their family's reputation unsullied."

Mika nodded, but then echoed what Santi had said earlier. "They don't seem like the "run you off the road" types, though, do they? They filed a formal cease and desist letter before. You think they'd just ramp up their legal strategy."

Now, it was my turn to sigh because as much as I really wanted someone to pin my fear and anger on, I knew they were right. This didn't feel like Solomon Sumner's way of doing things. "Okay, but then who?"

"Let's talk through this strategically," Mika said as she pulled a small notebook and a pen from her purse. "What exactly about you might be threatening to someone?"

I pretended to flip my hair over my shoulder and said, "My scathing intellect, my profound beauty, my excellent research skills."

"Definitely all of those things," Mika said with a grin, "but I think it's probably the latter one that might be the most dangerous to other people, right?"

"I don't know about that," Santi said as he squeezed my knee under the table.

I blushed but turned back to Mika. "So someone is worried what I'll find as I look into what? The Sumner family history?" I quickly flipped through my recent salvage and research projects, but I didn't come up with anything even remotely controversial except the Sumners. Most of my work involved tracking down the species of wood or the age of glass, not the reasons for murder.

"Like I said, I think so, Paisley. Why do you doubt that?" Santi's voice was even, but I could tell he was getting a little frustrated with my skepticism.

"To be honest, I'm not sure." I sat a minute and let my mind tunnel into what I was feeling about the situation. Why *did* I doubt it would be the Sumner research?" I sat a minute, and then, like a jolt, it hit me. "It's because no one else knows except Mark and Mariah." A cold sweat broke out on my skin when I said that.

"Knows about what?" Santi asked. "The whole county knows about Lily because you wrote about her in your newsletter."

"Sorry. Yeah, not that. No, I found some photographs and a journal hidden today." I couldn't believe I hadn't told Santi about this yet, but I filled him in now. "But no one but Mark and Mariah know what I found."

"You don't think it's them, do you?" Mika asked quietly.

I shook my head, trying to convince myself as much as to convince Mika and Santi. "Why would they care? It's not their family history, and they brought me in to do the research."

Santi nodded. "You're right, but we can't rule them out if they're the only people who knew."

"I hear you, but what would their motive be? To pay me less?" That just didn't sound like these two generous people who had invited me into their home.

"Are you sure they aren't related to the Sumners?" Mika asked.

I hadn't even thought of that. "I'm not sure because I never thought to look. Pass me my laptop," I pointed to where it sat on the island next to Mika.

She handed it over, and I quickly opened the genealogy site

I used and typed in Mark's name. Since he was alive, I wasn't sure how much information I'd find, but pretty quickly, I was able to track his family back a few generations, and all of them had lived in the Plains states like Iowa and North Dakota. No ties to Virginia.

Mariah's search was a little tougher because it took me a minute to find her maiden name, but soon, I could see that her people were all from New England. Virginia roots weren't in her tree at all, as best I could tell. "Doesn't look like they are related to the Sumners at all, at least not in recent history." We were all related if you went back far enough, but if we went back that far, the name Sumner probably wasn't even in use yet.

"Okay, so then that leaves us with Solomon Sumner or other members of his family that were more upset than we initially thought about the article on Lily," Santi said.

A thought occurred to me. "Or someone else who wants to protect the Sumners from, well, themselves," I said quietly.

Santi looked at me intently. "Anyone in particular?"

I sighed. "Well, if my family had worked for another family for generations, I might just feel I had something to lose if their secrets were exposed."

"Linda or Rob," Santi said with resignation.

"Yeah," I replied. "Linda seemed okay today after the passageway incident, but then maybe that was all an act. And I didn't see Rob today at all."

Mika looked from me to Santiago and then back to me. "You think the employees might be protecting their former employers?" She shook her head. "I've worked for lots of people, and while I've liked most of them, I've never felt my loyalty extended to covering up a murder."

"But then, you haven't relied on your bosses for centuries of work," I said.

"True that," Mika said. "True that."

10

When it became clear we couldn't get any further with our suppositions about who had tried to kill me, Mika helped us clean up and then headed home. Santiago and I went back to the couch, where he watched some TV show about spaceships and I sank into my sewing and the up and down of simple black thread. Unfortunately, every time I felt myself relaxing, the nagging question of who wanted me dead would poke itself up into my consciousness again.

Eventually, though, I had to get some sleep, so we went upstairs and climbed into bed, where Santiago held me close until I drifted off. Sometimes, the body does work we can't do for ourselves, and I slept like a baby for eight hours before waking gently to sunshine on my face and the smell of coffee.

Santiago set the mug next to me and said, "I'm glad you slept." He kissed my cheek and then sat down on the bed. "How are you feeling?"

I stretched and checked in with myself. "Rested, which is good, but still scared, you know?"

He put his hand on my cheek. "I do know. Does it help to know I'll be with you all day?"

I grinned. "It always helps when you're around. You're coming with me to the Sumner's?"

"I am. Figured I'd park my cruiser at the road and then walk up and help you look through things. If that's okay with you, that is." He held out a hand to help me sit up and then placed my coffee mug in my hand.

"Totally okay with me." I frowned. "Do Mark and Mariah know you're coming?"

"They do." He held up his phone. "I just texted Mark and told him about last night."

"Oh." I took a deep breath as my heart sped up. "Was that smart? I mean, if he chased me...."

Santiago pulled me against his side. "If he chased you, then he already knows, and if he didn't, he can help keep you safe. He's going to work entirely from home today just in case."

A little swoosh of relief passed through me, and I decided to trust myself. If my first instinct was to feel safer with Mark around, then there was probably something to that. "Okay. Sounds good."

It didn't take us long to get ready and eat a little cereal, and soon we were on the road up to the Sumners. When Santiago pulled up to the house to drop me off, I was surprised to see several cars already in the driveway, several cars I recognized. Dad and Lucille's car was there, as was Mary's. Saul's truck was parked along the back. "You brought reinforcements?"

"Your dad brought reinforcements. I talked with him this morning, and he insisted. Said they could help with sorting things."

A small grin slid onto my face. "Of course, he did. So much for a productive day though?" My dad was great company and super good at lots of things like woodworking and gardening, but the kind of detailed attention that came with my work wasn't his forte.

"Actually, Mark asked if he and Saul could help him with a project, so they'll be here and out of your hair." He grinned at me.

"What kind of project?" I said as I stepped out of the car.

"I've been sworn to secrecy," he said as he took my hand. "But you'll like it."

I shook my head. "Always scheming, you people," I said and smiled. "And Mary?"

"Oh, she's here to help you, and Lucille is making some sort of something in the kitchen for Mariah. I think pie crust is involved." Santi waggled his eyebrows. He loved my stepmom's pie.

"Well, I guess we should go in and play our parts in the great Sumner House Extravaganza of... whatever is going on." I was confused about the situation but not displeased. I loved my people, and I loved that they wanted to be near me today.

Santiago steered me away from the front door and around the side of the brick house. As we approached the backyard, I could hear voices, and when I turned the corner, I saw all of the people I loved, including Mika, standing around with coffee mugs in their hands.

I walked over to my best friend and said, "How are you here?" Normally, she needed to be in her store most days, especially after her big expansion and new website. Her sales were booming, but she wasn't at a place yet where she could afford full-time help.

"Oh, you know Mrs. Stephenson. When she heard what happened, she insisted she take over the store today so I could be with you." She hugged me tight. "I admit I didn't put up much of a fight. You okay?"

"I am, mostly. I'd actually just like to get to work and forget about last night." I looked around. "After I get some coffee that is."

Mika smiled. "Good to see you have your priorities straight." She walked me over to a low brick wall by the back of the house and poured a cup of dark, rich goodness into a green ceramic mug before adding French vanilla almond creamer and giving me the cup.

I took a slow sip and then my eyes fluttered closed in delight. "It's delicious."

"Glad you like it," Mariah said as she joined us. "It's from the roastery just over the mountain. Organic, fair trade, small-batch."

"All the things I love in coffee and delicious, too," I said as I clinked my mug against hers. "Thank you." I looked around. "Thank you for all of this."

"Are you kidding?" she said. "When your dad and stepmom said they wanted to spend the day here and asked if we could use some help with anything, we were delighted. And now that you have more help," she looked from Mika to Mary, "We're even happier. It's going to be a good day, Paisley."

I forced my smile wider and then said, "Well, are you ready to get started?"

Mariah nodded. "I'm going to be in the kitchen with your stepmom. She's promised to give me a pastry lesson, but Mika, you, Mary, and Santi are with Paisley, right?"

"That's right," Mika said and slipped her arm through mine. "Let's gather our team and get to work."

I waved to Dad, Lucille, Saul, and Mark and then headed toward the back door of the library to let us in. I figured we'd make our plan there and then head up to the bedrooms and go systematically through any drawers and closets there. Mariah had mentioned a suitcase of old letters in one closet, so I thought I'd start there with Mika. I asked Santiago and Mary, who held me tight in a hug when we got inside, if they'd begin with the drawers in that same room.

With everyone given their research orders, we started to work, and soon I found myself completely lost in the process of pulling out letters, checking dates and names, and then organizing the findings into various piles for my shop, the historical society, or the Owenses place.

Across the room, Santi and Mary did the same, occasionally holding up an old makeup compact or handkerchief to ask me what I wanted to do with it. Our process was slow and deliberate, and when I finally looked up at the clock, I found two hours had passed and we were almost done with this room. Many hands really did make light work.

Mid-morning, Mom and Lucille called us down to the dining room for more coffee and the apple tarts they had just made. The pastry was flaky and the apples tangy and sweet, and I ate two of them before I even thought about it.

As we sat around and talked, I heard Mariah and Lucille talking about plans for a bakery subscription service. Apparently, they were thinking people would subscribe for six months of baked goods and then be delivered something new every week. I didn't have the capacity to get all the details at the moment, but I knew my stepmom had been wanting to start a baking business of some sort. Mariah as her partner seemed like the perfect fit.

With my second cup of coffee in hand, I made my way over to where Dad, Saul, Mark, and Santi were talking, and when I asked what project they were working on, Dad took me by the shoulders and led me outside to the edge of the garden, where I could see the frame of what looked to be a very nice and large pergola taking shape. "They wanted a place to sit in the shade and enjoy the garden," Dad said as Saul joined us. "What do you think?"

I ran my hands along the grayed beams and said, "It's beautiful." Then I looked at Saul. "Are these the posts from that barn up in the hollow?"

"Good eye, Paisley girl," he said. "Mark came by the lot yesterday afternoon and picked these out. A couple of my guys will be here soon with the rafters from that same barn. She's going to be a beaut."

"You didn't charge him for this did you, Saul?" I asked. The Owens had given me so much already that I felt guilty asking them to pay for the materials for such a small project.

Saul winked at me. "Mark and I knew you would say that, so we worked a deal. Instead of paying you for the wood, he made a donation to the high school to help them build a new greenhouse for their ag program."

I grinned. "Oh, I love that," I said. While I had a formal college education, I knew a lot of folks, including Santi, didn't really care for all that "book learning." But they did need skills and jobs, and so I was glad to help out with the agriculture training at the high school.

As the guys began talking about beam lengths and fasteners, I wandered over to a low bench that overlooked the barns and the fields below. I could see why the first Sumners had built here. The view was spectacular, especially on a clear day like this one.

Down below, I saw Rob on a small red tractor. He was pulling a bushhog along through one of the fields. The trailer bounced along behind him as it mowed down the tall grass in the field. As he turned the machine and came back toward the house, he looked up, and just in case he saw me, I waved. It felt like he saw me because his gaze stopped in my direction, but he didn't wave back. Just kept on mowing, focused on his job.

I set my coffee mug on the ground and laid back on the bench and closed my eyes. The stress of the past few days was wearing me down, and I relished a moment to simply rest as I let my mind wander over the past few days, I felt that niggling sensation I always got when my brain was putting together information faster than I could process it. I knew better than to try to force any revelation and simply took a few deep breaths and let the sun warm my face.

Before I could get too sleepy or sunburned, I stood up, grabbed my mug, and headed back inside. Everyone else was still milling about with pastries and coffee, and I thought I'd take the chance to figure out our next room before Mika, Mary, and Santi came back in.

After depositing my mug in the kitchen, I went back into the dining room and decided to take the secret passageway up to the second floor, just for kicks. The dark hallway was getting less and less spooky, but no less cool, each time I used it, and I tried to imagine myself as an enslaved woman moving between the rooms.

As I climbed the small staircase to the second floor, I lost my balance a bit and leaned against the railing to steady myself. Beneath my right hand, I felt a small knob of wood sticking out from the rest of the smooth beam, and out of instinct, I pushed my finger into it. A click caused me to step down one stair as a slim wooden drawer slid out from the wall beside me.

There, inside the drawer, I saw something golden that shimmered in my phone's flashlight. I reached down and took out a pocket watch with a long chain. The outside of the case was etched with fine filigree, and inside, the mechanism looked brilliant, even in the limited light. This watch was valuable, I knew right away.

Eagerly, I slipped the watch into my pocket, pushed the drawer shut, and turned around to go find Mariah and Mark. They needed to know about this find right away. I bustled down the stairs and out into the dining room, where I found Linda and Rob having a very quiet conversation in the corner by the kitchen.

When they saw me, they both stopped talking and studied

my face. "You were in the passageway again?" Linda said, her voice a bit uneven.

"Just enjoying the Nancy Drew feel. I loved those books." Something told me that it wasn't wise to share my new finding with these two. "I had to decide which room we were going to go through next and decided to use the passageway to get there."

Rob's lips turned up into a slim smile. "And which room are you going through?"

Since I hadn't even made that decision yet, I paused for a split second before saying, "The red one at the front. That huge dresser might be full of goodies." I tried to smile as brightly as I could, even though the tension in the room had just gotten palpable for reasons I couldn't explain.

"Good plan," he said. "That was the first Mr. Sumner's bedroom. Who knows what you'll find?"

A shiver crossed over my arms as I thought about the pictures of the old man dead in his bed with his wife posed next to him. "Who knows?" I said. "Always more mysteries to uncover in these old houses," I said as I waved and headed out the back door, my hand gripped tightly around the watch.

Santiago intercepted me before I got to the larger group. "Where were you?" he said, his voice full of concern.

"Sorry. I should have told you. I was just going to pick our next research room." I lowered my voice, "but I found something on the way." I took his arm and led him a bit further from the house. "Linda and Rob are inside, and—"

"They are," Santi's voice grew sharp. "Mariah said that Linda had taken the day off, and I just saw Rob mowing down below."

"Me, too," I said, "But they're both inside now, and they saw me come out of the secret passageway." I turned my back a little more to the house and then held the watch out in front of me.

"I found this in a secret drawer in the passageway staircase. It seems valuable."

Santi glanced down at the watch and then up at my face. "They didn't see it did they?"

I shook my head. "No. I was coming to tell Mark and Mariah."

"Let's just keep this to ourselves for now. Maybe get an expert to look at it first before we start sharing the news." Santi's voice was quiet but clear. He was in sheriff mode.

"Okay. You take it then. I don't want to risk having it fall out of my pocket while I work." I stepped closer to him, kissed his cheek, and slid the watch into his front pants pocket all at once.

"You've got the moves, Ms. Sutton," he said, as he bent down to kiss me on the lips. "You've got all the moves."

I chuckled, feeling a little of the tension in my neck release. "Only for you, Sheriff Shifflett," I said.

He pulled me to him and whispered in my ear. "I'll just run this to town and get Savannah to check it out. Stay close to Mika and Mary. I'll be back soon."

I nodded against his shoulder and then let go. "I can't believe they did that," I said a bit too loudly.

Santi looked at me with a question in his eyes, but then seemed to get it. "Me neither. Seriously, you'd think it would not be such a big deal how the flower pots in town got watered, but apparently, they've come to near blows and need a moderator. I won't be long."

I snickered. The huge hanging baskets in town were a continual source of small-town controversy in Octonia. People fought over everything from the choice of flowers to when they should be hung and taken down and even about how they should be watered – with gray water from the town buildings or fresh water from the stream. Those flowers were as clear an indicator as any that some of the people of Octonia needed a little more to do with their spare time.

But our ruse was effective, given that it was just as likely Santi would have to mediate a flowerpot dispute as it was anything else, so with a wave, he headed off, and I grabbed my two girlfriends and took them inside and upstairs, through the main part of the house this time. I didn't see Rob or Linda anywhere now, but I didn't feel like dealing with that hostility I'd felt the last time they'd been nearby.

I really wanted to tell Mary and Mika about the watch, but something told me it wasn't a good idea to talk about anything I didn't want overheard in the house. So instead, we just buckled down and giggled over the various things we found in the drawers of Mr. Sumner's bedroom. Some old-fashion underwear, shoe polish that looked to have been made from actual tar, and a fair number of romance novels with very risqué scenes tucked into the back of the drawers. Someone liked steamy romance but didn't want anyone else to know they did.

We packed the things of worth into a tote I'd brought along and then set out the rest for Mariah and Mark to peruse before donating it. That room hadn't yielded much for me beyond a beautiful silver hairbrush set and a pitcher and wash basin, but I wasn't complaining. This job was, by far, my most lucrative yet, and I was so grateful to the Owens for the work.

With only one more room to tackle, the women and I decided to continue and see if we could make a good start on this last room before lunch, which smelled amazing. This last bedroom was the smallest, tucked into the back corner of the house, but it also looked like it had become a sort of catch-all for the house. Boxes filled the corners, and the closet was absolutely stuffed with, well, stuff.

Each of us took a spot on the floor and began to tackle a different stack of boxes. I claimed the closet and began by pulling a jewelry box out of the top corner. Jewelry boxes had been rich with surprises before, and I was hoping the same would be true now. When I opened the top and saw compartments full of costume jewelry – or at least what I thought was costume jewelry – I gave a little woot. My customers loved antique jewelry, and I had developed a pretty good process for identifying the maker's marks and pricing the pieces. This would be a good afternoon's work for Mary and me one day.

Mary had become my sort of research assistant in lots of ways. She still worked part-time as a nurse, but as my business had begun to grow, I'd begun hiring her to help me find out information about various pieces and grow my online store as well as my in-person shop. She was very thorough and detail-oriented in ways that I just wasn't, and we made a good team. Nursing had been pretty taxing for her as of late, so I was really hoping I could bring her on full-time soon.

I held up the box to show Mary, and she grinned. "Yes, tea and research tomorrow?" she said.

"Sounds perfect. Can we work at your store, Mika?" I loved being in my friend's yarn shop, and while she was often too busy with customers and classes to help us do much investigation, I knew that Mika enjoyed having our company there.

"Of course you can," Mika said. "Look at this." She held up what looked like a christening gown. "The monogram is SS."

I sighed. "Oh, that must have been baby Simon's gown." I studied the tiny dress. "Please set that aside, and I'll see if Solomon wants it. That should stay in the family." Mika nodded and carefully draped the gown over the bed beside her.

For the next half-hour, we each dug into our piles, moving items into piles and showing each other particularly interesting finds. We were discovering a lot of old pieces, including a gorgeous mantel clock that just needed a good tune-up to get working, and we were also helping the Owens make this into a functional guest space. It always felt nice to do good work for good people.

And I couldn't help but think the Owens were good people. I knew that Mika and Santi were right, and we wouldn't completely dismiss any possibility of suspicion from them. But given that they had been nothing but nice to me, I was having a really hard time imagining either of them driving me off the road. Besides, I hadn't seen either of them in a large black SUV.

It was just about lunch time, and I had stood to suggest we head down for whatever heavenly-smelling lunch Mariah and Lucille had whipped up when Linda came into the room beside me and closed the door. "Did you take it, Paisley?" she said in a whisper.

I stared at her for a minute, too confused to answer.

"Did you take it from the stairwell drawer?" she asked again, her eyes flicking back and forth around the room.

"What are you talking about?" I finally managed to say as my brain caught up and I flashed through the best courses of action here.

She took a deep breath. "It's gone, and he knows. You were in there. Did you take it?"

I studied Linda again and shook my head. "I have no idea what you are talking about. What stairwell drawer?" I was a terrible actor, but I hoped Linda believed me.

"Are you sure? Because he's very angry, and if he finds out you have it?" Linda's eyes were wide as she stared at me, and I thought of Beau and the way he looked at me when he really wanted tuna. It was a pretty manipulative look, I had to say.

"I don't know what you're talking about, Linda," I said as calmly as I could. "What is missing?"

Linda looked from me to Mary to Mika, and my friends looked just as confused as I hoped I did. "Yeah, what's missing?" Mary asked.

"Never mind," Linda said with a wave of her hand. "I just thought—" She looked at me again. "Never mind. Forget I said anything." With that, she turned and walked out the door.

My heart was beating a million miles a minute, but I took a deep breath and looked at my friends. "That was weird," I said as I did my best not to lie to these people I loved while becoming more determined than ever not to bring them further than they already were into whatever this was.

"So weird." Mika said as she looked carefully at my face before saying, "I'm famished. Let's eat." I couldn't be sure, but I felt pretty certain that my two friends knew I knew something, but they also knew better than to ask. I loved them all the more for that.

We made our way downstairs and found Lucille and Mariah in the kitchen behind a spread of sandwich makings that would rival the best sub shops in the world. Besides the variety of veggies, and meats and cheeses, it was the two kinds of sub rolls that stole the show. One was dark and heavy, a pumpernickel, I thought, and the other was covered in toasted cheese and had, I found when I cut it open, cheese melted throughout the bread. If each roll hadn't been eight inches long, I would have definitely sampled both.

But I made do with my cheese bread and filled it with all the veggies and cheeses I could. When Santiago returned just after I finished, I resoundingly suggested he try the pumpernickel and then turned on my heel to go to the dining room, confident he had taken my hint.

He had, and when he sat down with his meat-filled bun, I immediately tore off a corner of the bread and tried it. It was, undoubtedly, every bit as good as my own bread. But since mine had cheese in it and was, arguably, on my plate, I restrained myself and ate my own food... with occasional thefts from Santi's plate.

I was dying to know what he'd found out about the watch, but I didn't want to ask in front of everyone and I wasn't sure he'd even know anything new yet. Savannah would probably have to take the piece to Charlottesville to get it appraised, and that would take a couple of hours at least.

Still, I did need to tell him about Linda confronting me

about the drawer and what was missing from it, so when we finished eating, I suggested we take a stroll through the garden. Everyone at the table snickered as we stood up, and I could tell they thought "stroll through the garden" was code for "make out by the green beans," but I didn't dissuade them from their beliefs. Who knew, maybe we would.

But first, I told Santi about Linda's strange query and about how I had, hopefully, played it off. "So she knows you took it?" he asked.

"She suspects I took it, but she seemed most concerned that Rob knew," I said as we turned around the cantaloupes and made our way back toward the house.

"Rob knew about what?" A voice said from behind us. There was Rob himself, standing at the edge of the garden with a handcart behind him. "Did you guys need something?"

He seemed so easy-going and friendly, that I almost slipped and told him about the watch, but fortunately Santi squeezed my hand and said, "About what Mariah uses to keep slugs off her melons."

I kept my eyes on Rob as if I had known exactly what Santi was going to say, but inside, I was so impressed with how quickly he had come up with that response. "Slugs get my melons every year, and it looks like Mariah's are doing great. What is the secret?"

"Two actually," Rob said as he set the cart down by the cucumber vines. "Diatomaceous earth and beer bait." He pointed toward the Styrofoam bowls whose tops sat flush with the ground. "Slugs love beer, so they climb in and drown. Any that aren't aching for a drink get cut up by the diatomaceous earth that she sprinkles out each evening."

"Excellent," I said, actually making a mental note to try those things for the very real slug problem I had. "Thanks."

"Anytime." Rob tugged his cart closer and began to put dozens of cucumbers inside. "Mariah has the greenest thumb I know, and we're all grateful since she shares the bounty with all of us."

I smiled. "That is awesome. Who doesn't love cucumbers?"

Santiago raised a hand.

"Besides you, weirdo," I said. "Thanks for the tips, Rob. I better get back to it."

He waved and then went right back to picking cucumbers.

"Either he's the coolest cucumber in the world," I whispered to Santi, "or that man doesn't know a thing about that watch."

THE REST of the afternoon sped by as three of us sorted all the materials in that room, hauled out two huge boxes of papers for the historical society – mostly church bulletins from the Episcopal congregation the Sumners had been a part of – and loaded the back of Santi's cruiser with several boxes of things for me to sell, including that great jewelry box and a couple of old quilts Mika had unearthed from a box. I was very, very tempted to keep those for myself, but I knew they'd fetch good money in the shop, especially since they looked to be hand-sewn.

After Mika and Mary left, escorted by Saul and Dad and Lucille, Mariah, Mark, Santi, and I took a seat under the now-completed pergola. It wasn't a completely shady spot yet, but it still felt lovely to be in the semi-shade with the breeze coming up off the river. When Mariah handed us each a mint julep, it felt like the perfect end to a very good day.

But unfortunately, we hadn't stayed just to relax. Santi wanted to talk with the Owens, see if they knew anything about the secret drawer or the watch, and feel out, a little more deeply, whether they had anything to do with the SUV that attacked me the day before.

Before Santi could even broach the subject, though, Mark

said, "Paisley, we are so sorry about what happened to you yesterday. We completely understand if you would rather not do any further work and would prefer to sever our relationship now." His eyes were sad when he spoke, but I could hear the sincerity in his offer.

"Also," Mark continued as he turned to Santi, "given that Mariah and I should definitely be considered as suspects, I took the liberty of having the DMV send your Deputy Wilson all our registration information so that she could check it against the description of the vehicle that attacked Paisley."

Santi smiled. "She told me, and I appreciate that. We definitely checked your information and see you have no such vehicle, and I checked your alibi with Saul. He says you were with him at exactly the time Pais was attacked." He turned to Mariah, "And Belinda said you were in the garden until well after dusk."

I looked from him to my new friends. "Oh, thank goodness. You have no idea how much I wanted to know you were innocent." I smiled and hoped they could hear my relief.

"We are glad we can prove that, for your sake as well as ours," Mariah said as she briefly reached over and clasped my hand. "I can't imagine how terrifying that was for you, probably still is."

I sighed. "It was scary, but I was glad to know I could still drive like a bat out of hell when necessary."

My friends chuckled, but then Santi grew serious again. "Did you two know there was a secret drawer on the stairwell of the secret passageway?"

Mark and Mariah looked at each other and then back at us. "No. A secret storage spot within a secret passage – that seems like a lot of embedded secrets," Mariah said.

I nodded. "It is, and I found the drawer by accident today when I decided to go upstairs through the passage, just for fun. I can show you where it is."

"Let's do that in a bit," Santi said, "but maybe you can tell them what you found there first." He looked at me and nodded.

If the sheriff wanted me to share something, then I definitely would because he was a wise law enforcement officer but also because I trusted him explicitly. "A gold pocket watch. A very fine one, I believe."

Mariah's brow furrowed. "Someone hid a pocketwatch in a super-secret compartment. Why would they do that?"

I shook my head. "Maybe it's very valuable and someone wanted to keep it safe?"

Mark sighed. "Possible, but why not just put it in a safety deposit box, or even a safe here in the house?"

"That's exactly what I've been wondering. Savannah took the watch down to an expert in Charlottesville. He's going to appraise it and see what he can find out tonight, so we'll know more in the morning," Santi said.

"This is all getting so weird. First the two gravestones. Then Lily's escape and Mrs. Sumner's murder of her husband. Now a strange pocketwatch in a secret drawer." I sighed. "Even Nancy Drew didn't have this much mystery to deal with."

"You think Nancy Drew, I think Scooby Doo," Santi said as he stood and helped me to my feet. "Show us where you found this drawer?"

The four of us went into the house and then through the door in the dining room and into the passageway. I led the way to the stairs and then climbed slowly, feeling for the little knub of wood that was the button as I went. Just almost exactly halfway up, I felt it and gave it a little push. The drawer swung open, and the four of us stared at it for a moment.

"Wow," Mark said as he leaned over the drawer with his phone flashlight. "That's remarkable."

"It really is," I replied. "The craftsmanship alone, and I can't imagine what the mechanism is that allows it to open from over here on the other side of the stairs." Spatial understandings were not my forte, and this one really baffled me.

"Do you think slaves hid things here? Maybe passed messages?" Mariah's voice was hushed.

I hadn't thought about that possibility, but it made a lot of sense. "Could be. If an enslaved carpenter created this staircase, then maybe he put in the drawer, too."

"I wonder if there's any indication of this on those drawings I found," I mused out loud.

"Oh, good question. Let's go look. I just got them back from the framer," Mark said as he turned and led us back down the stairs. But when he got to the door, it was closed and wouldn't budge. He let me come forward to give the latch a go, but it wouldn't move.

"We've been locked in," I said as I felt my pulse begin to pick up.

"Let's go check the other doors, and if all else fails, at least we know where the secret door is," Mariah said efficiently and then marched off toward the front of the house.

It didn't take long to find that all the doors were locked, and we headed for the fireplace on the second floor. I reached over and pulled the lever that Linda had shown us, and it creaked but didn't move down like it was supposed to. The firebox didn't swing outward.

I tried again, but still nothing. "You try," I said to Santi, putting his hand on the lever and showing him how to pull down. Still not a budge.

"Maybe it's stuck," Mariah said and put her shoulder against the back of the coal stove. The sucker didn't shift a millimeter. It was fine and wholly locked shut.

We were completely trapped.

. . .

I'M NOT someone who suffers with claustrophobia, at least under normal circumstances, but it turns out that when you are trapped in a passageway that almost no one knows about, claustrophobia can set in pretty quickly.

And apparently, I wasn't the only one who felt it because within moments of us realizing we were locked in, both Mark and I were on the steps with our heads between our legs and our partners coaching us to take slow, steady breaths. That helped, and once we were calm, Santiago said, "We have cell signal, so we won't be in here long."

Then, he walked a few steps and called Savannah. "She's on her way," he said, "with backup."

I nodded and then put my head between my knees again. My mind was spinning. Linda and Rob had both been here earlier, so they could have locked us in here. But why would they do that?

"Let's go check the doors again," Mariah said, and we dutifully tramped off behind her. I clutched Santi's hand like it was my portal to hope because, well, it was.

The doors were all still locked shut, but this time when we went to the door at the back bedroom of the house, we could hear something. It sounded like thumping, like someone was moving furniture. But in the tunnel, I couldn't get a clear sense of direction or amplitude. We could have been hearing someone hammering down on the railroad track or someone making a bed in one of the bedrooms.

Eventually the sound stopped, and the four of us settled to the floor to wait for our rescuer. I thought about trying to start a conversation, seeing if we could piece things together again. But I just didn't have the energy, and since no one else seemed to feel much like talking either, we all sat silently, our backs against one wall and our feet pressed against the other.

The panic was just starting to set in again for me when I

heard a loud clunk downstairs and then the sound of Savannah shouting, "Sheriff, Paisley, where are you?"

Santi quickly stood and leaned over the stairwell. "We're up here. Bedroom right above you. Can you make it to us?"

"Yep, just a second." I heard her footfalls as she jogged across the house to the front stairs and then back over to us. Then, another clunk, and the wardrobe swung open. "Here we are. Come on out," she said.

Even though we'd only been in the space for a half-hour at most, I still had to shield my eyes from the late afternoon sunlight when we came out. The sun was dipping into the trees now, and soon, we'd be into the part of the day that mosquitoes loved most.

For a few moments, we all stood in the bedroom, getting our bearings and regrouping. Mark looked quite pale, but his eyes were sharp. And Mariah looked the same as when she'd gone in, or maybe a little better since it seemed like she had enjoyed the adventure. Santi, however, was mad as a rooster, and I didn't want to be at the end of his spurs when he figured out who had trapped us in there.

Savannah took a look around while we gathered ourselves, and in a couple of minutes she came and said, "I think you should all see this."

We followed her out the bedroom door and down the short hall to the room where Mary, Mika, and I had been working today. It was completely turned over. Every box, every bin dumped, and even the mattresses pulled from the bed.

"Oh my gracious," Mariah said as her hand flew to her mouth. Claustrophobia hadn't gotten to her, but breaking and entering certainly had.

"This is why they locked us in," Mark said with certainty. "To give themselves time."

Santi nodded. "Looks like it. Keep anything valuable in this room?"

Mariah looked at me. "Paisley, you'd know better than I would what was in here."

I shook my head. "Nothing valuable. Most of this is just bedding or contemporary books," I said pointing to a jumble in the corner that had been neatly folded and stacked an hour ago. "And this over here was sewing supplies, fabric, trims and such that I was going to suggest Mark and Mariah donate to the church quilting bee."

I scanned the room one more time. "The rest was just stuff, lamp shades, extra kitchen utensils, that kind of thing. We already loaded up anything valuable from in here, but even that stuff wasn't particularly special." A thought snagged in my mind. "I did find a jewelry box though. I thought it was probably mostly costume jewelry, but maybe something more valuable was in there."

Santi looked around the room. "Maybe. But that jewelry box had been there, presumably, for a long time, right?" He looked from Mariah, to Mark, and then to me.

The three of us nodded.

"So it seems like the burglar would have come for that a long time ago if they'd known it was here." Santiago began strolling around the room. "But today, they took a huge risk, locked us up, and then looked for something while we were indisposed. Why?"

At the same time, Mark and I said, "The watch."

Santi and Savannah looked at the two of us. "The watch," Santi said. "That must be it."

"Someone went to this much trouble to find an old pocket watch?" Mariah asked.

"Not just any old pocket watch. Julius Sumner's pocket watch. It's worth a might, especially since the workings inside are laid in with diamonds and other gems. The appraiser will give me an official value tomorrow, but he suggested that it might be worth a few hundred thousand dollars," Savannah said.

"What?!" Mark said. "A watch that expensive was just tucked into a drawer in the wall."

"Tucked into a secret drawer in a secret wall," I said. "That's a pretty good hiding place if you don't want someone to find something."

"But why hide it like that?" Santi asked. "If it's that valuable, wouldn't you want to protect it? And maybe even show it off from time to time? I've never heard of this watch. Have any of you?"

We all shook our heads. If something this expensive was known out and about in Octonia, we would have heard about it. The gossip mill here was nothing if not thorough. Now, that mill might have said the watch was made from diamonds that were harvested from the great pyramids of Egypt, but we would have at least heard of the watch. Since none of us had, that meant it had been kept hidden for a long time… and, it seemed, for a good reason.

"Looks like we have another mystery to solve," I said. "Maybe your watch friend can help us figure out more?"

"He'll be in touch first thing tomorrow," Savannah said. "And I'm sure he will be eager to hear anything we can find, too."

Santi nodded. "Okay, then. Mark and Mariah, the deputy will be out," he looked at his watch, "should be out at the end of your driveway now. I'll check as we leave. If anything at all suspicious happens, call us."

"Will do," Mark said as he shook Santi's hand.

The couple walked the three of us to the door, and I gave Mariah a brief hug before we headed out toward two police cruisers and a lot of questions.

11

If I hadn't been prone to car sickness, I would already have been looking into watch histories as we drove. Instead, I began to make a mental list of avenues I could follow when we got home. First, Santi wanted to go pick up my car. He didn't want to leave it at the station any longer, and he also wanted us to have two vehicles should we need them. I didn't have the energy to ask what he thought we both might need a car for and just rode along.

After I drove the cruiser and Santi drove my car, at his insistence, I set out leftovers on the counter, grabbed a hard cider, and opened my laptop. I had to figure out what this watch meant. I began with what I knew – that the watch had belonged to Julius Sumner. I scanned all the newspaper articles and other public records I could find about him, and finally, in a sketch in the local paper dated just a year before his death, I saw the pocket watch, or at least its chain, trailing from his vest pocket. Sumner had been a man of means, for sure, but I doubted he had enough means to warrant two pocket watches. It seemed that this was the one we'd found.

I dialed Savannah as I continued to tap at the keyboard

while Santiago heated up dinner for us. "How did your expert know the watch belonged to Julius Sumner?" I asked as soon as she picked up.

"Hello to you, too, Paisley," she said with a laugh. "The watch is engraved with his name inside the back of the case."

"Ah, got it. Thanks." I hung up without saying goodbye.

My next call was to Ms. Nicholas. I needed her extensive knowledge and research skills to see what else we could learn. I told her about the watch, about what we knew of it, and asked if she could please search the records tonight to see what else she could find. I knew I was asking a lot of someone whose salary was barely enough for her to pay her bills, but she readily agreed and said she'd be back in touch by 10 p.m.

Then, as I ate leftover pizza, boxed macaroni and cheese, and some cucumber slices that Santi had insisted we add from the garden -- "We need a vegetable," he'd said – I began to construct a timeline for the watch based on the Sumner family trees, what I knew of heredity patterns among the wealthy, and the tiny bit I had gleaned about the relationships between the Sumner family members.

When I was done with what I could surmise, I found Santiago on the front porch and dropped into the rocker beside him, a sheaf of papers in my hands. "Want to hear my sort of half-baked sort-of-researched theory?"

"Sure, as long as you know I can't act on half-baked," he said as he took my hand into his. "Hit me. "

"Okay, so I think that watch has been passed down to the oldest Sumner son in each generation ever since old Julius himself died." I showed Santiago my family trees and then the way that the wills, which I had copied from the courthouse early on in this project, showed each oldest male inherited the family land and the "gold pocket watch" as it was designated in the documents.

"If I'm right, then the last person to inherit that watch was Solomon Sumner." I took a breath and looked at Santiago.

He stared out across the field for a minute and then looked at me. "Do you think Sumner locked us in the passageway to toss the bedroom and find his watch?"

I shrugged. "I don't know. That still doesn't seem like his style, but it would make sense. He probably knew about the locks and the escape route through the fireplace, don't you think?"

This time, Santiago looked befuddled. "I don't know exactly what he knew, but it does sound like it's time I talk with him and get some answers."

I pulled our hands from his lap to mine. "Can it wait until morning? I've had enough excitement for the day."

He kissed my fingers. "Yes, it can definitely wait until morning. By then, we'll know more, too."

We spent a bit more time on the porch with Beauregard, who decide the papers in my hand were clearly intended as a bed and laid his giant girth across all of them and my legs while he snored... loudly. It was a good thing I loved him... and that he had claws.

Eventually, though, I tipped the fuzzy boy off my lap and invited the not-as-fuzzy boy inside to watch TV while I sewed. This time, he opted for *Long Way Round*, the Ewan MacGregor motorcycle show that satisfied both of us – him with the bikes and me with MacGregor. I got a few hundred more stitches into my blackwork, which I was really loving and thought might be something I could do more quickly for gifts and such.

I tried to tell myself I was always too ambitious with sewing projects, but tonight, for some reason, I felt like I could do anything.

. . .

THE NEXT MORNING, Santiago and I took it slow with coffee on the porch while the robins danced around the yard. It was a gorgeous day, not tending to be too hot it seemed, and I sort of wished we could just lounge around here, do some wedding planning, and take naps.

But Savannah called with news from the appraiser right at 8, and by 8:15 we were on our way to meet him at the coffee house in downtown Octonia. Apparently, whatever he had to share was pressing and required a face-to-face.

When we arrived downtown, Savannah was already at a table with a tiny man who had the largest moustache I'd ever seen over very pale skin. He looked a bit like Gollum had a baby with Luigi from Mario Brothers, and I could not wait to meet him.

With our lattes in hand, Santiago and I went to the table and introduced ourselves. "Sheriff, Paisley, this is Hudson Salmanara, an antique watch expert. He has a lot to tell us about the Sumner Watch."

We sat down, and Mr. Salmanara began right away. "This is a famous watch, well, famous in watch circles. It was made in 1844 by a famous maker in Geneva for Julius Sumner. That's evident from the presence of Sumner's name in the casing itself but also from the maker's logbook, which has been preserved."

I didn't say anything, but I was impressed both by this man's research and by the fact that a record of watches made 175 years ago still existed.

"The watch is well-known because of its unique style. It's made of eighteen-karat gold, which isn't that rare, but the internal clock face, which you can see here," he unfolded the watch from a piece of very soft-looking material and opened the back," is mounted with rubies and diamonds."

"Why put the gems where most people wouldn't see them?" I asked.

"A good question, young lady," Mr. Salmanara said. "It was a way of flaunting wealth without, well, feeling like you were flaunting it. You see, most men would simply remove their watch to look at the time and then slide it back into their pocket. But with a watch like this," he spun the piece so the front faced us, "as soon as he removed it and opened the cover, anyone near him would see the fine craftsmanship on the case and the dial. Then, they might have asked to see the watch altogether."

"And then, they would have opened the back to see the gems," Santiago said. "It's a bit like having a massive house on a hill behind the trees. The only people who can see its grandeur are those who are invited to witness it."

"Exactly," Mr. Salmanara said with a smile. "But this watch is also famous for another reason."

"Oh," I said as I leaned forward. "What reason would that be?"

Mr. Salmanara leaned in as well, and his voice dropped to a whisper. "The legend in the clockmaking world is that Julius Sumner gave this watch to his mistress only to have his wife find out."

I sat back hard in my chair. "Really? Is there any proof? Do you know who his mistress was?"

"No idea," he said, "but the story I've heard is that when Eliza Sumner found out, she killed her husband and the other woman."

Santiago looked from Mr. Salmanara to me and then to Savannah. "Well. That is a very interesting theory."

"One last question, sir," I said as Mr. Salmanara handed Savannah the watch and began to gather his other things. "Does that legend say anything about how Mrs. Sumner got the watch back?"

The old man winked at me, and I felt like I'd just been blessed by a wise old wizard. "Rumor has it that she tricked the woman into coming to their house on pretense of friendship, suggesting that perhaps the two of them might make amends if the woman brought over the watch to return. But Mrs. Sumner simply took the watch and locked the other woman in a secret passageway until she starved to death."

A wave of fear washed over me. There was too much in this rumor of Salmanara's for it to be entirely fiction. I stared at him a minute too long, and finally, Santi saved me. "Thank you for your time, Mr. Salmanara. Savannah will be sure to get you payment for your appraisal services, and we'll be in touch if we have other questions. Thanks again." Santi walked the older man to the door, and I waved to him as he walked back past the coffee shop window.

Then, I dropped into my chair and ran my hands back and forth over my face before looking at Savannah and saying, "Holy crap."

"You can say that again," she said. "That Eliza Sumner was something. Glad I didn't cross her."

"Amen to that," I said as Santiago handed me my latte mug that was full again. I was just trying to figure out how and if we could prove that story true, or false, as the case may be, when my phone rang. I dug it out of my pocket and answered right away. "Ms. Nicholas, did you find something?"

"I did, Ms. Sutton. Are you free to come by the Society soon?" she said in her calm, refined way.

"Santiago, Savannah, and I are just at the coffee shop. Is now a good time? And if so, can we bring you anything?"

Ms. Nicholas chuckled. "Well, I've been up all night, so if you saw fit to bring something with caffeine, I believe my body and I would be most grateful."

"You got it," I said and stood up. "We'll see you in five minutes."

I ordered Ms. Nicholas a huge latte with a double shot of espresso and also grabbed her a chocolate croissant since she likely hadn't eaten at all if she'd been researching all night.

Then, my two police companions and I walked the few blocks up the sidewalk to the former Victorian mansion that now housed the historical society offices.

Ms. Nicholas met us at the door and guided us, after a caution about being especially careful with our beverages, into the front room where she had laid out quite an array of images and papers. I was drawn, immediately, to the ones of various men wearing a pocket watch that, as best I could tell from a distance, was the one Savannah now had in her hand.

"You found pictures of men with the watch?" I said as I studied the lineup she'd put out.

"I did. There, they are in chronological order, oldest on the left, newest on the right." She slid a piece of paper my way, and I saw there the names of each man written with their dates of birth and death. I quickly pulled my own Sumner family trees and matched everything up. Clearly, Ms. Nicholas had been on the same trail.

"You found these images after seeing the wills?" I asked.

"Exactly," she said. "The clerk opened the records room for me first thing this morning so I could confirm."

Say what you will about small-town people being up in everyone's business, but we did a good job of helping everyone out when we could, too.

"Walk me through this," Savannah said, and for the next few minutes, Ms. Nicholas explained who each man was and to whom he had given the watch. "Finally, we have Solomon Sumner, the watch's current owner, as best the records indicate." She tapped one long, red fingernail on the picture of Solomon. To be fair, it appeared his grumpy face was just his normal expression.

"So do we think Solomon hid the watch in the secret drawer?" I said as my brain tried to put all these facts together.

Santi shook his head. "That seems too haphazard for him."

"Agreed," Savannah said. "I hadn't told you yet, but his

attorney came by to inform us that Solomon was seeking a restraining order against Paisley. He's trying to claim that she's causing him harm by researching his family's story."

I looked from Savannah to Santi to Ms. Nicholas and then back to Santi again. "I doubt it," he said. "Although a judge can pretty much order anything if they think there's cause." He turned to Savannah. "Who's on bench duty today?"

"Judge Warren."

Santi smiled. "You're safe for another day, Pais. Judge Warren has no need of fools."

I felt a little relieved but still mightily disturbed that someone would want to stop my research badly enough that they'd file a restraining order. But all I said was "Okay." We could worry about my legal troubles another time.

"What's next?" I said to no one in particular.

"Well," both Santi and Ms. Nicholas said at the same time.

"Ladies first," Santi said.

Ms. Nicholas smiled and moved toward the other side of the table, where she had laid out a collection of books and papers. "I think that one reason someone is hiding that watch is that it seems to have been linked to a couple of murders or disappearances, the ones you've been looking into, Paisley." Her face was very somber as she looked at me.

"We heard the rumor that Sumner had given the watch to his mistress and then that his wife, Eliza, had killed him and her for their affair. Is that what you're talking about?" I asked.

"Part of it. And it's no rumor, at least not the affair. This is MaryJane Reddy's journal," she tapped a red nail on a slim book, "and she records her affair with Julius Sumner in some quite extensive detail. She even describes the circumstances under which he gave her the watch."

I was dying to know all the details of, well, everything, but we had a more pressing issue at hand to deal with. "But you said the watch was also linked to a disappearance? Lily's disappearance?" My heart was speeding along again.

"Yes, if my hypothesis is correct, Lily stole the watch from the person who abused her and planned to sell it to fund her disappearance." Ms. Nicholas's voice was low and serious.

"But the watch is here, which means Lily didn't successfully sell it... or if she did, someone found it and bought it back..." My mind was racing, but I couldn't get the threads to weave together quickly enough.

"Or someone found Lily and got the watch back from her," Santi said quietly.

My heart jumped into my throat. "Oh no. She may be in danger," I shouted as I pulled my phone out of my pocket and dialed Mr. Bourne's number.

He picked up on the first ring. "Mr. Bourne, this is Paisley Sutton. Is Lily—?"

The voice on the other end of the line interrupted me, and it most certainly wasn't Mr. Bourne. "Lily is unavailable to come to the phone right now, Paisley. But if you'd care to meet us at the Sumner house in, say thirty minutes, I think we can answer all your questions and some of mine."

A chill pitched down my spine. "Linda, is that you?"

"I'll see you there in 30, Paisley. Don't bring your friends." She hung up.

SAVANNAH AND SANTIAGO stared at me, and I stared at my phone. "That was Linda?" Santiago asked as he gently lifted my chin to look at him.

I nodded. "She says I have to come to her now, alone." I looked into Santi's eyes. "I think she has kidnapped Mr. Bourne and Lily."

Santis' eyes grew wide. "Where does she want to meet?" He already had his phone out.

"Santi, she said I had to come alone." I didn't like that idea at all, but I liked the possibility that she might hurt Lily or Mr. Bourne even less. "I can do this."

Santi pulled me to his chest. "Of course, you can, and you will go alone. But we can't let you go without some sort of backup."

I shuddered against his chest. "Okay," I whimpered.

"Savannah, you got plain clothes with you?"

"Sure do, Sheriff. I can be there in ten minutes." Her voice was sure.

"Perfect. Drive your personal car, too," Santi was still holding me with one arm, but I could feel him dialing with the other. "Saul, I need you and the Suttons at the Sumner Place ASAP. Just go to work on the pergola. But stay close."

"Okay, so now your backup will be in place." He held me at arm's length. "Let's talk about what you're going to say."

I took a breath to steady myself and then said, "I'm going to figure out what in the world is going on." I looked up at him. "If that's okay."

"That's more than okay, baby," he said. "But we'll be close by and listening. Go and head on over. I'll come in the back way and get close to the house."

I started to walk across the street to my car, but then I thought of something. "What about Mariah and Mark?" I said as I turned around at the edge of the sidewalk.

"I'll call them on the way, and don't worry about them. With a little forewarning, they'll be your best allies in there." He blew me a kiss and then jogged off toward the sheriff's office.

If my mind hadn't been buzzing already, I might have pondered Santi's comment about the Owens a little more deeply. But at the moment, my body was already overwhelmed with all the things I had to manage, including my own growing fear.

· · ·

SOMEHOW, though, I managed to make the drive to the Sumner Place without incident, and when I parked my car out front, I would have thought it was any other day if I hadn't just been scared to death over the phone.

As I walked toward the house, I imagined snipers on the roof or someone watching me from the front windows with a pistol trained on my head. But since I didn't see any of the tell-tale flashes that always gave the killers away in movies, I hoped that meant I was safe and made my way to the front door.

It opened before I even knocked, and Linda stood in the doorway, a smile on her face that made the blood freeze in my veins. She looked stunned, like her face had gotten stuck in the kind of grin we all put on for photographs. It was terrifying.

Behind her, I could see Mark and Mariah sitting on the settee by the wall, and in two chairs near them, Mr. Bourne and an older woman sat clutching hands. That had to be Lily.

"I'm here. Now what?" I said, forcing as much aggression into my voice as I could muster in an attempt to mask my terror.

"Come in, Paisley. Please, make yourself at home." Linda stepped back from the door and allowed me to enter. As I walked past her, Mark gave me a slight nod, and Mariah smiled placidly, as if they were simply having tea with a friend.

And it turned out they were having tea. Mariah's glass pitcher of iced tea was set on the coffee table with five glasses. Linda moved toward it and filled each glass before handing one to each of us and pointing to the low-slung chair she had slid over from the other side of the room. "Please, Paisley, have a seat."

I tried to scan the room casually as I lowered myself into the seat. I didn't see any sign of a weapon, but who knew what Linda might have tucked into her belt or in the pockets of her cargo shorts. As she handed me my tea, I glanced over at

Mariah, who very subtly shook her head and looked at my glass. Guess I wouldn't be drinking that.

"Now that we're all here, we can begin our negotiations. Let's start with my first demand, shall we?" Linda sounded far more like an aristocratic Southern woman than the rough-handed landscaper I'd met a few days ago, and I had to say that the difference heightened the creep factor by a hundred. "I want the watch."

I tried to keep my face even as I looked at her. She glared at me. "I know you have it."

"I don't have it," I said, a true statement in every sense of the word. "But if I did, it doesn't belong to you. It belongs to Solomon Sumner."

She practically hissed as she said, "Solomon. That man is a monster. I know you know that, Lily. But you've always been too cowardly to confront him." She stared at Lily, who, to her credit, didn't look away.

Linda turned back to me. "That watch is what's owed me after keeping all this family's secrets my entire life. My father won that fair and square in a poker game, but Solomon was too much of a coward to give it up. Thought it might upset his daddy. Waa. Waa." The bitterness in Linda's voice was so strong I could almost taste it.

"The watch is yours, then," Mark said from behind where Linda was standing. "Technically we own it now since it was left in the house, and I'll gladly give it to you if it means we can end this nonsense."

"Excellent. Bring it to me," Linda said.

"I can't do that, but you have my word."

"Your word," Linda sneered. "The word of the people who own this house has been no good to anyone of us who work here. Not now and not ever."

Mark shook his head. "I am a man of my word, Linda. I'll even sign something, and you can have it witnessed by the people here if you'd like."

Linda rolled her eyes. "Fine, we'll come back to my first demand. Now, Paisley, I need you to commit to writing an article about my family for your newsletter. It won't be the respect we are due, but it will be something."

"Sure, Linda," I said. "I had actually thought about writing a piece on your family and Rob's family anyway. You've been so loyal to the Sumners all these years." Again, I wasn't lying. I had thought about the article, and if agreeing to write one got us all out of this mess, then I'd gladly do it.

"You can write about the Fords if you want, but the Roberts deserve our own article. We've been here longer." Linda's voice was pompous, and while I didn't doubt the factual accuracy of what she said, she sounded like a pouting four-year-old who had just lost a foot race.

"I can do that," I said quickly. "What else do you want?"

She turned to Lily. "I want you to come forward and tell the world what happened to you, not as Alexis Benfield, but as Lily Sumner. I want you to put Solomon Sumner in prison."

Lily's face had gone sheet white, and I saw Bourne grip her fingers more tightly. But when Lily spoke, her voice was steady. "What good would that do, Linda? After all this time."

Linda's face grew even harder. "It might not do any good for anyone but me, but it'll do me a world of good. If you had only spoken up when he first attacked you... "I heard Linda's voice crack, and she stopped talking.

And just like that, I understood. I wanted to get up and hug the woman standing before me, the one who had probably poisoned my iced tea and who had tried to run me off the road. Because in that instant, I knew she had been assaulted, too. "Oh Linda," was all I said, though.

She spun toward me. "Don't pity me. I overcame what that man did to me, and I didn't run and hide. I couldn't run. I had to stay and put up with it until he decided I was too old and he moved on." She glowered at Lily.

Mariah spoke quietly from her seat. "You were both little girls, both victims of a predator. Neither one of you did anything wrong by surviving in whatever way you could."

"That's not true," Linda said. "If she," she jabbed a finger at Lily, "had just spoken up, if she had told someone, anyone, then he might have gone to jail."

Tears filled Lily's eyes. "You thought I didn't tell anyone?"

Linda stopped and looked at the older woman, staring at her as a revelation of her own dawned. "You did?"

Lily nodded. "I did. I told my parents, but they didn't do anything. I was 11. I had no power. The only thing I could do was leave, and your mother and Rob's father helped me escape. Do you think they would have done that if there was another way?"

Linda sank down to her knees in the middle of the room. "My mother knew." The tears were trailing down her face now. "She knew."

Lily stood and walked to the younger woman, placing her hands in Linda's red hair and making soothing sounds like I used to get Sawyer to sleep as an infant.

"You didn't tell your mother?" I asked quietly, my brain trying to fit all these pieces together. "Why?"

"Because Solomon said he'd kill her." Linda's voice was mostly a sob now. "He said if I told anyone, he'd kill them and then kill me."

"Shhh, shhh," Lily said as she continued to stroke Linda's hair. "You did the best you could. You survived. That is amazing."

Linda sobbed into Lily's legs, and as she did, I watched Mark walk over, bend down, and take a pistol out of Linda's pants pocket. He quickly removed the bullets and put the gun on the other side of the room before whistling once.

At the sound, Savannah and Santiago came into the room from separate doors, both with their guns drawn. But as soon as they saw the scene, they holstered their weapons and walked toward me. "You okay?" Santi asked as he hugged me to his chest.

"I am. But Linda is not. Not at all." I couldn't feel anything but deep sadness for the woman who had been forced to carry far too many secrets for far too long. "Do you have to arrest her?"

Bourne stood from his chair and walked over to the three of us. "I think I can speak for both Lily and myself when I say we don't want to press charges."

I stared at the man who had been – just moments ago – kept against his will with, it now seemed apparent to me, the woman he loved and found tears welling in my eyes at his grace. "That's a very kind thing, Mr. Bourne."

"If there's one thing I've learned from my forty years of loving Lily Sumner, it's that trauma makes people do incredible things – sometimes good things and sometimes horrible. But all because we just want to heal." He looked over at the two women who were now sitting on the settee embracing. "It's not always the easy thing to forgive, but it's always the right thing for everyone, especially the person who was hurt."

I let his words settle into me deeply as I watched the two women embrace. "But Solomon Sumner?"

"Well, there is no statute of limitations on assault and rape in Virginia, so if Lily or Linda want to press charges, I can have him in jail by the end of the day," Santi said.

Lily pulled Linda out to her arm's length. "What do you think, Linda? Is it time we spoke up?"

Linda studied the older woman. "Yes, if you'll go with me."

The two women stood together, and Savannah escorted them into the dining room to get their statements.

"I'll get the warrant and have him arrested by nightfall,"

Santi kissed my cheek and went out the door to do the part of his job that gave him the most satisfaction and the most sadness.

Mariah said, "How does hot tea sound, maybe with a shot of whiskey?"

I smiled and said, "That sounds great. Do you mind if I go see my dad while you make it?"

"No need to go anywhere, darling," my dad said as he stepped in from behind the dining room wall. "I've been here the whole time, and I am so proud of you." He pulled me into his arms, and I melted into tears. All my fear gone and replaced with just sadness at all the pain that lived in the world.

As PROMISED, Santi had Solomon Sumner behind bars by nightfall. The older man hadn't put up a fight at his arrest, but when his slick attorney had shown up, Solomon was cautioned against saying anything at all.

But once the newspaper got word of the charges that Lily and Linda were pressing against Sumner, other women a little older than Lily and some as young as their late 20s came forward to add their charges to the case, and soon, it was apparent that no amount of fancy lawyering was going to keep Solomon Sumner from getting his due.

As an act of support, and with Linda's permission, Mark and Mariah sold Solomon's gold watch and used the funds to set up a foundation for sexual assault victims in Octonia. They hired professional counselors and provided training in schools and civic groups around the county to help victims have safe spaces to speak up and be heard.

It turned out, as I learned after questioning Mark incessantly one night a few weeks after we were held hostage about his skills with a gun – "You unloaded that thing like you'd done it a hundred times" – that he was former FBI and so was

Mariah. But since they'd come to Octonia to live a quiet life, I kept their secret, well, from everyone but Mika and Mary because there were no secrets among dear friends.

I did write up the article about Julius and Eliza Sumner and her murder of her husband and his mistress. Between Ms. Nicholas and me, we were able to uncover enough primary source evidence to be decisive in our determination that Eliza Sumner killed two people in her lifetime, but our first surmise, that she had lived with postpartum depression after the birth of her child, seemed to still be true. But whether that illness led her to kill her son Simon or whether he died of natural causes, the world will never know.

The story of the murders was big news in Octonia, and if Solomon Sumner hadn't already tarnished his family's reputation beyond repute already, it might have even been the scandal of the fall. But with so many victims and so much support needed in the community, the news of 150-year-old murders wasn't that much of a splash.

I made enough money from my work with the Owens and the auction they held in September to be able to put away a big chunk of cash for Sawyer's education and spring for a fancy honeymoon in Alaska, a place Santi and I had always wanted to go.

But before we could escape to the northern wilderness, we still had a wedding to plan and hold and a whole community to keep informed of our plans, whether we wanted to or not. Octonia had always been and probably always would be the land where gossip spread like dandelion seeds, and I wouldn't have wanted it any other way.

Read the next of Paisley's adventures in *Aida Time* - https:// books2read.com/aidatime.

FREE STORY

*If you'd like to read about Harvey and Mart's adventures at the Johnson Ranch, **download your free story here:** https://dl. bookfunnel.com/6kcevcn3il*

Happy Reading! - ACF

ALSO BY ACF BOOKENS

St. Marin's Cozy Mystery Series

Publishable By Death

Entitled To Kill

Bound To Execute

Plotted For Murder

Tome To Tomb

Scripted To Slay

Proof Of Death

Epilogue of An Epitaph

Hardcover Homicide

Picture Book Peril

Stitches In Crime Series

Crossed By Death

Bobbins and Bodies

Hanged By A Thread

Counted Corpse

Stitch X For Murder

Sewn At The Crime

Blood And Backstitches

Fatal Floss

Strangled Skein

Aida Time

Poe Baxter Books Series

Fatalities And Folios

Massacre And Margins

Butchery And Bindings

Monograph and Murder - Coming in March 2023

Spines and Slaughter - Coming in April 2023

ABOUT THE AUTHOR

ACF Bookens lives in Virginia's Southwestern Mountains with her young son, an old hound, and a bully mix who has already eaten two couches. When she's not writing, she cross-stitches, watches YA fantasy shows, and grows massive quantities of cucumbers. Find her at acfbookens.com.